Clive Towle was born in 1939 and is a retired mechanical engineer. He was called up for national service but signed on as a regular. He has done many things in life. He has written his life story, *The Life and Times of a Country Lad,* which has been published and is now a vintage tractor enthusiast.

Martin Blacker for his mobile crane pictures.

Wrawby Wind Mills for the photos of the mill.

Clive Towle

Surviving a Destroyed World with The Johnsons

Austin Macauley Publishers™

London • Cambridge • New York • Sharjah

A CIP catalogue record for this title is available from the British Library.

ISBN 9781035805600 (Paperback)
ISBN 9781035805617 (ePub e-book)

www.austinmacauley.com

First Published 2024
Austin Macauley Publishers Ltd®
1 Canada Square
Canary Wharf
London
E14 5AA

Acknowledgement

I must express gratitude to Kirsty and Kenny for granting me the opportunity to transform them into the unimaginable.

Susan Day for Wrawby Mill.

Martin Blacker

Preface

A story I first wrote and
pencil sketched in 1996.
(Art was never my strong point.)

When I first decided to write this book I wasn't sure where I would have the area located.

Then after some thought I decided to make it local. So the story area is based on, and around the north Lincolnshire town of Scunthorpe and southern area of the town. This is where I started in business and met lots of people.

Because I've known a lot of people I thought I would base all my characters on friends and people I have known.

None of the character's names are real, all names have been changed.

Introduction

After World War Three, a significant portion of the Earth had been ravaged, either directly by bombs or by subsequent radiation. However, in certain areas away from the bomb sites, many buildings remained intact and required minimal repair. Once the radiation levels subsided, there would be a massive cleanup operation for any survivors in these regions. This story focuses on one such area.

While some people had constructed their own radiation shelters, these often fell short of providing full protection, resulting in fatalities or severe radiation-related injuries. Nevertheless, amidst the survival efforts, an unexpected consequence emerged: mutations in various creatures, including humans, born within these substandard shelters.

The Johnson family, who owned a farm, had constructed an unusually large shelter and brought some of their animals with them when the war began. However, peculiar occurrences transpired during the latter part of their sheltered existence. With their children having grown up and left home before the turmoil began, Farmer Johnson and his wife found themselves alone in the shelter for an extended period.

One day, while checking his radiation metre, Farmer Johnson noticed that it indicated clear readings outside. His wife, however, remained cautious, hesitant to take any unnecessary risks. After several days of consistent readings, Farmer Johnson eventually persuaded her to venture outside for a look. They emerged to find clear skies and sunshine, prompting a brief moment of enjoyment.

As they surveyed their farmyard about 100 metres away, they spotted a horse grazing near their farmhouse. Curious, they approached the animal, only for the radiation metre to sound warnings as they neared it. Despite this, they discovered that the radiation emitted by the horse was minimal, prompting them to lead it back to the shelter.

Upon returning to the shelter, the radiation readings ceased, leading them to speculate about the shelter's construction or its waste ejection system neutralising radiation in the vicinity. They remained indoors with the horse, aware that they had already been exposed to severe radiation.

Days later, the horse gave birth to a foal unlike anything they had seen before. Born during the night, the foal had the body and legs of a horse but the upper half of a human – a genuine centaur. Mrs Johnson, waking to this surreal sight, struggled to comprehend whether to call it a foal or a baby. Nevertheless, they resolved to care for the hybrid creature after it finished suckling from the mare, aware that its dietary needs would differ from the other horses. Amidst the pervasive radiation, they allowed the mare to breed with the other horses, knowing that the contamination rendered such distinctions inconsequential.

The farmer and his wife eventually passed away, but some of the animals survived, albeit with amazing differences. Somehow, the radiation had mixed up the genes of the humans and the horses, resulting in the Centaurs, as we now know them.

The Johnsons did live long enough to teach the new creatures to speak, and to do all the other things humans do because, after all, they were basically human with an extra bit on their back. So, this is how the new Centaurs came to be. They were very similar to the old Centaurs in Greek mythology, but these, having been brought up by humans, were good citizens as opposed to the mythological ones. They were so happy to be alive and well that they devoted their lives to doing good and helping any other survivors they may find.

The family of four Centaurs, dad Norman, mum Mary, and their children Tony and Beth, decided to keep the name Johnson which had been the farmer's, after all, they had more or less been their parents. Somehow Norman knew when the radiation had gone, probably because that was what had made them the way they were in the first place. They had waited a long time for the radiation to subside, but now they were out and ready to make a new life for themselves and encourage anyone else they find to do the same and make the best of what was available.

All kinds of mutants were wandering about, some were harmless and didn't bother anything, but others were quite aggressive and seemed to want to fight the world. Plant life was quite different, but the Centaurs didn't know what it looked like before, only what they had seen in pictures. So here they were in a brand-new world, because they had only known life in the shelter. They had the tools the farmer had owned and taught them how to use, and with the help of other humans who had survived perfectly, they decided, after some quite alarming meetings, to work together and build a new community.

The humans did take a while to get used to the fact that their neighbours were half horse and half human, but as the Johnson family spoke perfect English it didn't take long to adjust, as there were other kinds of mutants all over the place anyway. The human part of the Centaurs was more or less the same size as humans, but they were much stronger. And consequently, the back horse part was more the size of a pony but also had tremendous strength.

Although Norman had been brought up by the farmers and he knew what humans looked like he will never forget the day he first met another man, because humans had never seen him before.

Anyway, one day Norman was looking at some fruit on a row of small bushes, like a cross between gooseberries and brambles, and was wondering if they would be alright to eat when he saw a man walking towards him on the other side of the hedge. He realised that the man would have a bit of a shock when he saw him, so he had to think of something as the man was carrying a gun.

He bent down enough so just his head and shoulders were showing and before the man got to him shouted,

"Hello," the man stopped, "Good morning, how are you?" Norman continued.

"Oh hello, I'm fine thanks, and how are you?" replied the man.

"I'm very well," said Norman, "How long have you been out?"

"Only a couple of weeks," the man said, "how about you?"

"We've been out about six weeks but not too far away. We've been getting the garden sorted out so we can have some fresh vegetables."

They were more or less opposite each other now so Norman kept quite low behind the bushes.

"I was wondering if these were alright to eat." He said showing him the fruit but making sure he only exposed his head and shoulders.

"I think so," said the man, "my son had some the other day without asking me and he's still alright. By the way have you seen any of those short fat mutant creatures around here, they look a bit like a cross between a sheep and a pig."

"Not today," said Norman, "we saw one the other day but it ran off when it saw us."

"That's a change," said the man, "the two I've seen have tried to attack me but the gun changed their mind. I killed one but the other ran off, and it's excellent meat. By the way, have you got a gun?"

"Not with me," said Norman, "but I've three back in the shelter, and plenty of cartridges."

"You really should carry one with you, those things can be very aggressive."

Norman thought for a while then said, "By the way, I'm a mutant myself."

"Really, you don't look like one." The man said.

"Well I'm more or less the same as you and can do the same as you, but with a bit extra." Norman was a bit nervous, after all, the man did have a gun.

"How do you mean, a bit extra?"

"Well don't be too shocked, because I can assure you I'm perfectly all right and can be very helpful sometimes, I'll come round."

Well the man stared in amazement at Norman the Centaur, in fact he was quite speechless for a minute or so.

"I just don't know what to say," he said, "except, I'm Ted Pearson, pleased to meet you." And held out his hand.

"And I'm Norman Johnson." And they shook hands warmly.

"There's not only me either," said Norman, "I've got a wife and two kids back at the shelter, all like me, and we can do all the things you can, but even more," he added with a sly grin, "we can pull our own carts if we have to."

The two talked for about half an hour or so with Ted telling Norman he also had a wife and two kids until Ted said.

"Well it's been really nice meeting you Norman, but I must go now. I can't wait to tell the family about you. We must get together again soon, how about dinner sometime?"

"We live over that hill, about half an hour's walk past that big tree, on the edge of the village. That's half an hour for me, you might do it a bit quicker." He said laughing. And with his gun tucked under his arm he set off home. Then stopped and turned, "About dinner, how about Saturday, four o'clock at our place?"

"Sounds great," Norman replied, "as long as it's no trouble."

"No trouble at all, I'll come and meet you, bye."

Norman made his way back to the shelter where his wife was on the lookout for him returning, she always worried quietly when he was away for long, which was understandable.

He shouted when he saw her waiting for him, "I'm back."

"Is everything alright, what did you find?" she replied.

"Mary my love, everything is great, I think, and I also think it may be going to be even better."

"Oh, why," she asked inquisitively.

"We've been invited to dinner at a neighbour's place," he said.

"What, you're joking." she said.

"Certainly not," said Norman, "And what's more, we're going on Saturday."

"Well who are they, or even what are they?" Mary was getting a bit worried now, she was a shy person anyway, and this was getting to her already - a funny feeling in her stomach. Was she ready to meet other people, or maybe creatures similar to themselves?

"Well they are humans just like our parents were," said Norman.

"Oh I don't know, and how can we eat at the same table as humans, our tables are a lot higher than theirs will be, like Mr. And Mrs. Johnsons were," she was making excuses now.

"Don't worry Mary," said Norman, "there's a book somewhere about conducting yourself correctly towards others and I think there's a bit in it about eating out and entertaining."

Norman assured her that it would be alright, and when they told the children they were excited about it, except they weren't too sure how the human children would react to them, but being sensible teenagers they decided they could handle it.

So life went on at the Johnsons, Norman and Tony were busy in the garden, and Beth was helping mum Mary around the shelter which they still had to use as a home until a new house was built. Norman had done a few drawings and plans for a house but food was the most important thing at that time. They had cleared quite a lot of ground of weeds and rubbish and had a nice big garden where they had a good variety of plants. They had read the gardening books that the Johnson farmers had left and found that a lot of plants had grown back as normal after the radiation had gone. But there were a few that were quite different, like the fruit on the bushes Norman had been looking at when he met Ted.

The meat supply was quite good, as there were lots of the pig-like mutants wandering about, and Ted was right, they were good to eat. Mother Mary was always busy and Beth was just as keen to help her around the shelter, washing, cleaning, cooking and all the other things that women do in the home.

Mr and Mrs Johnson, the farmers, had been of the old traditional kind with old traditional rural values. Mrs Johnson had been a good example of the homely farmer's wife, and insisting her job was to look after the home and family and had been extremely proud doing so, and also helping with the farm livestock when necessary. Consequently, the Centaurs had been brought up in much the same way. Mary was enjoying her role as farmer's wife and mother and all the jobs that went with it, while Norman was happy to be the provider. It was as if time had gone back to the nineteenth century.

The male survivors were all going to have to be providers, being physically stronger; building, hunting for meat, gardening and as soon as possible, farming corn crops to make bread. This was not going to be a time for sexual equality or equal opportunities, it was going to be the survival of the fittest, or pull together and help each other.

The women were no less important, having to feed the family, keeping the home clean, listening to her husband's worries and problems, and comforting him in the evening when things were going wrong. After all, men are only stronger physically, most successful men have had a good woman behind them at some time. So really, anyone who had survived their time in the shelters was in with a good chance of making it on the outside.

One of the things that Mary really enjoyed, apart from fresh fruit and vegetables, was hanging the washing out in the fresh air. But cooking was her favourite. And strangely she had a brand new electric cooker! There were no shops to buy from but the farmers had thought of everything and took two new cookers into the shelter so when one was worn out the other would last until they came out, which is what happened. The other one had packed in only a few weeks ago. They also had a kit which contained all the things they needed to replace some of the solar panels that had gone down on the generator, so they were very well equipped.

Saturday came and Mary was quite worried about meeting the humans, and couldn't make up her mind which top to wear, and should they take something with them, because she had been reading the book about meeting people and read that you sometimes take a bottle of wine or something.

"Don't worry about it," Norman said reassuringly, "they won't be expecting anything because they know we are new to the world, and they were here before."

Ted had told Norman that they had been neighbours of the Johnsons before the war and had also been quite upset to learn that the Johnsons had died. But as the new Centaurs were now Johnsons, and been brought up by the farmers, they were going to have a lot to talk about.

Meanwhile, the Pearsons were almost as nervous about meeting the Centaurs. Ted was all right because he had already met Norman, so it was up to him to assure his family that there was nothing to worry about.

But Liz, his wife, was just as concerned as Mary and just couldn't begin to imagine what these 'horse people' were like, and was a bit annoyed at Ted for inviting them round so soon before she had a chance to get used to the idea. Too late now though, Saturday was here and the Johnsons were on their way.

"They should be on their way by now," said Ted, "I'll go and meet them, they don't know where we live."

"Can I come, Dad?" asked his son Peter.

"Yes of course you can, we're not going far, we'll see them coming down the lane." Jane wanted to stay with her mum, she still hadn't come to terms with 'horse people'. Young Pete had tried to reassure her because although he was two years younger he was very protective towards her.

"There's some horses over there." Peter had spotted something.

"No that'll be them," said his dad. "I'll go tell Mum." Pete was gone.

"Hello again Norman," said Ted as the four approached.

"Hi Ted," replied Norman, "this is the rest of the family I told you about. Mary, this is Ted Pearson."

"Hello Mary, nice to meet you."

"Pleased to meet you too," said Mary, shaking his hand.

"And these two are Tony and Beth," said Norman.

"Well let's go and find my family then shall we?" said Ted. Liz heard them coming and appeared sheepishly at the door to meet Ted with the Johnsons just behind him.

"It's alright Liz, come and meet our new neighbours."

With handshakes all round and the youngsters, Pete and Jane already busily chatting to Tony and Beth, the first meeting looked like being a great success.

Mary was the first to break the silence strangely enough by saying, "If you would like to go for a long walk one day we could give you a lift home if you got tired." Everyone laughed and that was it, the tension had gone and it looked like being an enjoyable party.

Ted had had his own engineering company before the war and had built an excellent shelter for his family but only big enough to house them and any children that might come along. "It hadn't occurred to me when I asked you that it would be a bit cramped in our place for you so we'll eat outside, we often do anyway as the weather is usually good nowadays." Ted was trying to be as polite as possible and continued, "I've put the table on that raised slab, and I hope I've got it right in thinking that you stand up to eat."

Norman told him that he was quite correct and not to worry about anything he wasn't sure of because he was quite new to the world anyway.

So the afternoon went by with the Pearsons sitting on chairs on the higher level and the Johnsons standing on the lower level at the other side of the table. The conversation covered nearly every subject imaginable, the children were getting on great, comparing their education progress and talking about how they could get together again for playing games and doing what most youngsters do. Mary and Liz really liked each other and found that they enjoyed much the same things, especially the cooking now that they had fresh things to cook instead of the survival food and what they had been able to grow in the shelter. Norman and Ted were already starting to make plans for the future about building new homes, the shelters were quite adequate but after being in them for so long they longed for a nice new house.

So the party went on into the evening, they had enjoyed a bottle of champagne that Ted had kept for this very occasion. "I've waited a long time to open that bottle," he told Norman, "and we've really enjoyed your company," as the Johnsons prepared to leave.

"Well, we've more than enjoyed being here and meeting you all, next time it's our treat," said Norman, and Mary added, "Don't worry tomorrow Ted but the table we still have Mrs. Johnson's."

"Well I'm busy tomorrow Ted but shall 1 come over on Monday and we can talk some more about the buildings we have in mind."

"Great," said Ted, "see you then." The children said their goodbyes and off they went home.

When they got back to the shelter, Norman sensed something was different. Everything seemed to be alright, but he knew someone had been there. It was almost dark, but in the dust around the garden, there were footprints. As they obviously weren't theirs, they had visitors. Then they saw the note on the entrance to the shelter; it just said 'sorry we missed you, we'll call again.' This set Mary off worrying again.

"Everything is all happening too quickly for me," she said. But Norman put his arm round her shoulders and said, "Mary, there must be hundreds of other people out there somewhere, and chances are that we will meet some of them sometime. We got on all right with the Pearsons, didn't we?"

"Yes, I suppose you're right, sorry, let's go to bed; that champagne has made me quite tired."

So there was something else for them to think about, but it was nothing a good night's sleep wouldn't cure.

"Goodnight Mum, Dad," said Tony and Beth together, "It's been a great day, hasn't it?"

"Certainly has," said Dad, "Goodnight."

Next morning they were up early as Dad said, it was going to be a busy day. There was a batch of vegetable plants to be planted in the plot they had prepared, the potatoes needed weeding and hilling to keep them covered. The potatoes had grown more or less the same as they had done before, possibly because they had been underground and reproduced themselves each year without a problem at all. Anyway, with a little attention from Norman, they had some really good potatoes growing. Tony had been picking some of the fruit Norman had found the other day on the bushes where he had met Ted, and got back about the same time as Mum was shouting them in for lunch.

"I've made a salad today," she said, "and hard-boiled eggs from the hens."

The hens were also much happier out in the open air, scratching about and finding much of their own food, but Norman had a job keeping them off his garden. After lunch, Jane did the dishes for Mum, and Tony had another try at the radio that had heard someone trying to reply but it always faded out.

"Dad, what do you think if I try to extend the aerial somehow? There's some more of that lightweight tubing in the back cupboard."

"You can try it if you like, son," replied Norman, "there must be more than us with a radio."

Mary was outside admiring her husband's garden when suddenly she came running into others.

"What's wrong?" asked Norman, "there's someone out there, behind those trees."

Mary helps Tony in the garden

23

She said, "It's not animals because I heard them laughing. I'll go have a look," said Norman, "coming, Tony?" As they got a bit nearer the trees from two ways, the lads had nowhere to go so they tried to crouch down and hide.

"All right, you might as well come out now we can see you," said Norman, approaching them from the other side.

Well, you can imagine what two young lads of that age were thinking with a Centaur on either side of them; they were trembling when they crawled out from under the bush.

"What are you going to do with us?" said one of them.

"We could eat you, what do you think, Dad?" said Tony jokingly.

The boys started crying.

"He's not serious," said Norman, "We want to be friends, would you like to come back to our place and meet Tony's sister and have some of our fruit? Then maybe you can tell us what you are doing here and where you come from."

The lads cheered up a bit, then smiled and said, "You won't hurt us, will you?"

"Of course not, and I'm sorry I made you cry. You can ride if you like."

"Oh, great," the lads said.

Norman and Tony lifted the boys onto their backs and headed back to the shelter. Once back at home, the boys jumped down to meet Beth and her mother.

"Hello, you two," said Mary, "you're lucky you didn't get yourselves shot; you could have been mistaken for mutants. You must be more careful in future."

Mary was being the typical mother that she was, worrying about youngsters. Well, the lads started telling them their story of how they came to be there. It appeared they had been watching the Johnsons for a couple of days. The boys had been the first to see them, then on the second day, their parents had come along with them to see for themselves but had been too afraid to approach them. The boys were twins and they had a sister two years older called Caroline.

"You haven't told us your names yet," Jane asked.

"I'm John and he's Carl," said one of the boys who looked very much alike.

Then Norman pointed out that their parents would be worried about them and that they should be going home, to which they agreed. They had told them where they lived and Norman realised that they had quite a way to go and suggested that they should have a ride home.

"Really, Oh! Thanks Mr. Johnson," said one of them.

The ride to their place didn't take too long at a steady trot and Norman wasn't too worried about meeting the Websters because they had already had enough courage to come to their place yesterday, but had unfortunately missed them.

"Mum, we're home," shouted the one on Norman's back as they got to the Webster's shelter. "Mr. Johnson's brought us home, you know, where we went yesterday."

A woman's shape appeared cautiously at the doorway, but didn't speak.

"Hello, I'm Norman Johnson," he said, "it's alright, we do speak English."

"They are really nice." said one of the boys. "Are you alright, Mum?"

"Er, Oh yes," she said, not quite sure what to make of the fact that her two sons had just been brought home on the backs of some creatures that were half horse and half human.

"Sure you're alright Mrs. Webster?" Tony asked.

"Er, yes, sure I'm fine, really, it's not every day you have your kids coming home with such unusual company. Although we saw you from the trees yesterday I didn't realise you were quite like this, I'm sorry, I must sound quite rude."

"Not at all," said Norman, "in fact we were all extremely worried about how the real humans would react to us. Our, I suppose you would call them 'adopted' parents, brought us up to believe that we may be the only ones of our kind, so we knew it wouldn't be easy."

"Well it's really good of you to bring the boys home, I was beginning to get worried, by the way, my name's Margaret, oh and here's my husband coming back, he's been looking for them," she waved to him to let him know all was well and shouted. "It's alright Harry, the boys are here."

"I know they are," replied the man, "I saw them coming and wasn't sure what was happening so I hid in the bushes until they had passed, and as I heard them laughing and talking I knew they were alright, and I followed them home, thanks for bringing them, and by the way I'm Harry Webster," he said to Norman and Tony who in turn introduced themselves.

"Where's Caroline?" asked Harry.

She appeared shyly at the door not quite sure what to make of it all, she hadn't seen the Johnsons before, she had stayed home studying yesterday when the others had gone out.

"Hello," she said quietly, but gave a slight smile when Tony winked at her. "The boys have probably told you we have seen you from the trees, one day last week, but only got up the courage to come and see you yesterday, but you were out, so we knew what you looked like." Harry admitted they had been spying on them but explained that they had wanted to know how the Johnsons had got through their time in the shelter, but when they had seen the centaurs they weren't sure what to do.

"Well this may come as a bit of a surprise, but you are only the second family we have met but you both knew the original Mr. and Mrs. Johnson."

"Really," said Harry, "and who are the others?"

"Ted & Liz Pearson, over in the other direction," said Norman, "do you know them?"

"Not personally but I've heard of Ted's engineering business, how are they?"

"They're fine," said Norman, "listen, why don't we all get together one day and have a good chat, I'm meeting Ted tomorrow. I can fix a date if you like, when is a good time for you?"

"Let's see, today is Sunday, so if we say Friday that will give us time to get a few ideas together to talk about."

"That's OK by me," said Norman, "but if Ted can't make it I'll let you know, I assume my place is alright so neither of you have too far to travel."

"That's fine by me," said Harry.

"We'll be off then," Norman said, "Mary will have dinner ready, bye, see you Friday."

It seems there was a misunderstanding. Let me make the necessary adjustments for you.

The Centaurs felt much better now that they had met some humans and actually made friends with them. They never believed it would be as easy as that, but still not sure what they were saying about them after they had gone.

But Norman assured his family that whatever anyone said, it didn't matter, but both the families they had met so far had seemed genuine enough.

The week went by with Norman and Tony keeping busy in the garden and beginning to get all the tools and other equipment unpacked from the storage units so they would know what was available. There was a good section of joinery tools, which had belonged to Mr. Johnson's brother, who had unfortunately been killed in an accident just before the war.

Mr Johnson had been a fairly good joiner in his own right as well as a farmer, and what he had taught Norman before his death was going to be very helpful in rebuilding their future.

Mary and Beth were busy, between household jobs, unpacking boxes of material for making clothes and bedding, but there was going to be much more than they would need, so they could trade some with other families, but they would need some new curtains for the new house as Beth pointed out.

The week went by and Norman, with Tony's help, got out the table they had always used. It was a big old traditional farmhouse kitchen table, but it was ideal for entertaining. At the end of it Norman had placed their own higher table, and the floor in the shelter was on two levels, the old table was on the higher level and the top finished up at the same height. Norman had seen Ted on Monday and they had had a good talk about all sorts of things, and Ted had said that Friday was OK and they would all come over.

Mary prepares some food for the men

Friday morning arrived, and Mary and Beth had already begun preparing the food, while Norman selected some of his finest vegetables from the fridge. By the way, the fridge was a new addition stored by the farmers along with the cooker. Norman had been returning from Ted's place when he came across the pigs, thankfully he had his gun with him. None of their pigs were ready for consumption, and they had opted to reserve the hens they had for eggs until they bred enough chicks to have them for food. Before the war, some of the farmers had convened to decide which animals to bring to their shelters due to space constraints. Consequently, the Johnsons had settled on horses, pigs, and chickens, while another farmer friend had opted for cattle and sheep. There was only so much space available for animal quarters. The other farmer lived quite a distance from the Johnsons, so meeting them was a future prospect to look forward to.

The Websters were the first to arrive, warmly greeted by Mary and Beth, who had already met the twins. Margaret introduced herself as a doctor and had served as the local G.P. in the town, while Harry had been a bank manager and chairman of the town's football club. The Pearsons arrived shortly thereafter, leading to more introductions all round. The children dispersed to play or explore, with Tony vigilantly watching out for any potential dangers. The girls got along famously, with Jane asking Beth if she would like her tail plaited, inspired by a book about horse shows. Beth eagerly agreed, enjoying the chance to be adorned, while Caroline joined in by brushing her coat. Meanwhile, the boys spent their time discussing their aspirations for adulthood and recounting how they had been assisting their fathers.

Thus, the gathering continued, with the men making numerous plans about rebuilding their lives and constructing new homes, while the women discussed their preferences for the new houses, the variety of foods available, and the best ways to utilise the materials Mary possessed. They conversed for hours until it was time to depart. Norman inquired if they would manage going home as it was getting late, but they reassured him they would be fine, as they would reach home before dark and had both brought their guns along. Everyone had thoroughly enjoyed the day and agreed to reconvene in the near future, bidding farewell as the Pearsons and the Websters embarked on their journey home.

Norman and Ted kept in touch regularly, and Norman had been getting used to all the tools that old Mr. Johnson had left. All the power tools were electric, running off the solar supply, but they had to be used sparingly as it was only a small solar system mainly for lighting and some cooking. Ted also had a good supply of tools; being an engineer, he had made sure he had all the equipment necessary for the jobs that had to be done. But first of all, Norman, Ted, and Harry, after a meeting one day, decided that it would be better to try to find out how many others had survived. Then, they aimed to gather as many people together as possible to discover what skills they had between them. The nearest bomb that had dropped to their area was over 100 miles away, so the houses were all still standing, but many were in need of quite a lot of attention.

Norman differed from the rest in this respect, as he had never lived in a house and obviously couldn't, so he was going to have to build his own. It would have to be a purpose-built building to accommodate their extraordinary physical condition, so they would have to stay in the shelter for quite a while yet. Ted and his family, however, had already started cleaning out their house. A few of the windows were broken, but Ted, like a few others with a bit of forethought and a shelter, had stocked up with things they would likely need when it was all over, like glass! As the war had looked like it was getting ever closer, people had had time to do a few things like that, those who had shelters, that is. Ted lived in the village which was about two miles from the Johnsons' farm, but Norman did most of the travelling to and fro' because it was obviously much quicker for him.

Tony went with his dad on the day they had arranged to take Ted into town where he had his workshop, and to see if two of his workmen had survived in their shelters. Being honest, he didn't really believe they would have because they only used the DIY kit that had been available at the time. Norman took his cart with him for Ted to ride in when they went, and when Ted's son Peter saw Tony, he pleaded with his dad to let him go too. So, with Norman pulling the cart with Ted and Pete in it and Tony trotting alongside, it was town next stop.

It was only about three miles to the industrial estate on the outskirts of town where Ted had his business and had been chatting to Norman about it. But after about twenty minutes, and getting close to the edge of town, Ted was suddenly very quiet.

"What's wrong, Ted?" asked Norman. "Have you seen something?"

"No, that's the problem," Ted replied. "I'm used to seeing things moving, people, cattle in the fields, traffic on the roads. But look at the roads, overgrown in places. They were always clean and tidy. I'm not sure if I'm quite ready for what we'll find when we get there."

Ted's business premises were about halfway down the first avenue of the estate off the main road. He couldn't speak; he just stood there in the gateway, looking.

"You know, Norman," he said, "it's just like I thought it would be."

His key opened the office door without too much trouble, and inside was exactly as he had left it. Outside, his truck was still standing there by the diesel tank, mobile crane parked in the corner.

"Let's try the workshop door." Ted was coming round a bit now, but the lock on the up-and-over door was not going to open. "Never mind," he said, "we'll go through the office."

The communication towers he was building still stood there, like they were waiting for the next shift to arrive, except for a bit of extra rust.

Ted showed Norman and Tony around the rest of the place and explained a few things that were obviously new to them. They hadn't seen anything like this before, nor had his son Peter. After an hour or so reminiscing and trying to decide what was going to work again and what wasn't,

"We'd better be moving on soon if we are to make the other calls we planned," said Norman. "We've quite a bit to do."

"You're right," said Ted. "I want to see if Jim and Allan made it."

They had been the two employees that Ted had known to have built shelters, but only small ones at home. The two men had lived near each other in a fairly new residential area on the southeast of town, with Allan the nearest and Jim about half a mile further on.

So, Allan's was the first stop. He had dug up his garden and built his shelter down in the ground because, as his house was situated, that was his only option and he had used one of the DIY kits. They arrived at Allan's house with Ted still experiencing this eerie feeling with nobody about and nothing much moving. Round the back of Allan's house, his shelter was all quiet; the door had not been opened, and there was no reply from the intercom. They checked the intercom was working by the voice reply feature, a bit like an answerphone. It records your message in the building, so if anyone is alive in there, you know they must have heard it when it is played back to you. If you don't get a response, you can only assume they didn't survive. Ted tried it again, still no response.

"Got to be moving on, Ted," Norman said quietly.

"Yes, yes, of course, let's try Jim."

Jim was only six or seven minutes from Allan's house on the way out of the new estate on a hillside. He had used a similar shelter to Allan but, being a bit more of a perfectionist, had added a few extras and basically made a much better job of it. They turned into the lane on the way up to Jim's, and Norman stopped.

"What's wrong?" said Ted.

"I saw something moving over there behind the hedge," replied Norman.

"Hello, who's there? This is Ted Pearson, who's that? Is that you, Jim?"

They stood there for a minute or so, then a man appeared through a gap in the hedge.

"Ted, is that really you?" Jim said.

Ted jumped down off the cart and ran over to Jim and just hugged him.

"I never thought we would ever see each other again," said Jim. "But what the hell are they?" Pointing at Norman and Tony.

"Not what, but who," replied Ted. "Let me introduce you, Jim. I would like you to meet Norman Johnson and his son Tony."

"Am I dreaming? Are my eyes playing tricks on me, or are you two real?"

"They're real enough," said Ted. "And they're all right, but don't ask any more at the moment, it's a long story."

Norman held out his hand. "Pleased to meet you, Jim," he said.

"Pleased to meet you too," Jim said, shaking his hand cautiously.

"And you too, Tony."

"And this is my lad, Peter," said Ted.

Jim had been out about a month and told them he had been over to see if Allan was alright and had got the same result, so they were fairly sure it was bad news there.

"I was wondering about the syndicate crowd," said Ted. "Have you been over there?"

"No, Jean doesn't like me to go too far on my own, but we have got a son now, Mike, he's seven," said Jim. "Let's go and meet them, but I'm not sure what they'll think of your two mates."

"They have seen some mutants wandering about, but I'll go on in front and warn them there's nothing to be afraid of."

"OK," said Ted, "but we can't stay long. We've got a long way to go yet, and we want to get round to the police station and check on Jack Bright and his syndicate before we go home."

They met Jean and Mike and chatted for a while, checked that they were in radio contact with each other, and arranged to meet up again in the near future.

A lot of the town was built on a hillside, as was the police station, and the cells had been built into the hill to the rear of the building, making an excellent choice for the shelter, and a great conversion job had been done.

Their arrival at the police station was met with as much welcome as Allan's house.

"Doesn't look good," said Ted, "nobody about."

"Let's find out," said Norman.

The main door to the reception area was closed, but not locked, and the door to the shelter was at the back just past the reception desk. Ted went in and tried the intercom, nothing.

"Try again, Ted," Norman had followed him in.

"OK, once more. Hello, is there anyone alive in there? This is Ted Pearson."

A few seconds passed then the reply came back.

'Hello, is there anyone alive in there? This is Ted Pearson.'

"Well, that looks like that then," said Ted, turning for the main door, "come on, Norman, let's go."

Ted was halfway through the door with Norman just behind him.

"Hold it a minute, Ted," said Norman.

"What is it?" said Ted.

"I'm not sure, but just listen for a minute."

They stood in silence for about twenty seconds or so, then, as if Norman had known it would, the intercom crackled into life again.

"Hello, who's out there?" came a voice from the speaker.

"They're alive," said Ted, and went back to the intercom. "It's Ted Pearson, is that you, Jack?"

Jack had been the local police sergeant before the war, and had known Ted fairly well.

"Yes, it's me, Jack, and am I pleased to hear your voice, what's it like out there?"

"It's alright, are you all OK?" Ted asked.

"Yes, more or less," came the reply, "we'll make a start opening up."

"Hang on a minute," said Ted, "It's getting a bit late now and we've a long way to go, so leave it until the morning and we'll see you then."

"Yes, OK, Ted, we'll see you tomorrow, by the way, who's we?"

"Oh, some friends I've met but we'll meet you all tomorrow, bye."

The four set off home quite pleased with their day, Ted with his workplace, then finding Jim, and finally finding the syndicate all survived had made the day quite successful.

Mary and Beth had gone over to the Pearsons for the day while Norman and Tony had been to the town. The men were a bit worried about leaving the women on their own, but Liz was quite handy with a gun should there be any trouble.

Beth trots out to meet her dad

The women must have heard them coming home, and Beth came trotting up to meet them as they arrived back at Ted's house.

"Everything alright?" asked Norman.

"Yes, fine," said Beth, "What did you find?"

"Well, we found some more people alive," said Norman, "but we'll tell you all about it in a minute."

Liz and Mary had prepared a meal for them when they got back, leaving enough time for the Johnsons to eat and get back home before dark.

The next day was going to be much the same plan; they were going to meet the others at the police station, and Ted wanted to call at his workshop and pick up a few more things for home. It was a bit out of their way, but Norman said he didn't mind. Ted had suggested that Mary and Beth came over and stayed with Liz again, and they had agreed. The women had decided that they would have a much better look round the village. They had been for a look round and seen a few things of interest, but tomorrow they would make a proper start.

The Johnson family arrived at Ted's house bright and early, and after making sure the ladies were in radio contact with them, the four set off once again for the town.

The ladies, however, after a cup of tea, started their tour of the village. They decided to start at the village store because it seemed to make sense that there would be at least a few things that would be useful.

The door was still locked with the closed sign hanging on the inside.

"We'll not break it," said Liz, "the boss only lived next door and I know where the key will be, I helped out here sometimes."

They went to the back door of the house; it was open. Liz entered cautiously.

"Careful Liz," Mary said, "you don't know what might be in there."

"I think it's alright, there's no foot marks in the dust."

There were no bodies lying around; they had probably died in bed. But that wasn't the job today; they just wanted a general outline of what the future was going to be. The keys were just where Liz had said they would be, and the shop door opened without much trouble. But, just as Ted had experienced yesterday, this strange feeling, and just couldn't speak for a few minutes. Time really had stood still; the shelves were still full of all the normal food, drink and cleaning things. Most of the stuff would be of no use at all, but some of the cleaning items would come in handy. In fact, Liz thought that some of the tinned food might still be worth trying.

Mary and Beth had never been in a shop before, but they had had fairly good schooling from the Johnsons. So Liz filled them in on a few of the things they didn't know. They had found enough bits and pieces to be going on with today: soap, polish, liquid cleaner, cloths and brushes.

"Why don't we claim the shop for ourselves," Liz said, "after all I did use to work here."

"Oh Mum, can we, can it be our shop?" said Jane.

"Well the owners didn't survive, and we are the first ones to get here, so why not?" Mary said, and took down a poster off the wall, turned it over, found a pencil that worked and started making her own notice:

TO ALL SURVIVORS
This shop is now back in business.
Please do not steal.
Contact LIZ PEARSON
10 Maple Avenue.
(Right at phone box, top of lane)

Liz smiled, "That's great Mary, but I doubt if anybody will take much notice of it, that's if there is anybody else."

"Why not?" asked Mary, a little surprised.

"Well not all people are as friendly as us, you haven't experienced the nastier side of the human race."

"Better be getting back," said Liz, "we can call at a few other places on the way, just for a look, then it'll be lunch time." Mary made sure her notice was in full view in the window, which she had cleaned, and Liz locked up again.

They walked back through the village, and Liz called at a couple of friend's houses just for a look through the window. Coming back to the gate of the second one which had belonged to a close friend, she was obviously crying.

"What's wrong Liz?" asked Mary.

Liz couldn't speak for a minute or so, then; "I'm all right," she sobbed, "it's just that I can't understand why."

"It's horrible, Kev and Pat, or what's left of them are still sitting on the sofa holding each other."

"I do understand," said Mary, putting an arm around her, "Mr and Mrs Johnson were our parents and we had to watch them die in much the same way. But we can't change what has happened, we have to look to the future."

"I know," said Liz, "sorry Mary, come on girls, let's move on."

They went by the local market gardener's place and wandered round the back.

"There might be some good vegetables," said Beth, "what's that cabbage looking thing over there Jane, it looks good?"

Jane pulled it up, and although it looked like it would be a very tender and tasty vegetable, it had potato-looking roots.

"How about that, Mum," she said, "two in one."

So that went into one of the bags on Mary's back.

"We'll try that later."

On the way back to the house, they had to pass the garage and filling station.

"We might as well have a look in here as well while we're here, I know Ted's got plenty of tools but we might just find something we need."

There was a car parked on the pumps and when they got to it they could see the remains of someone still sitting at the wheel. The workshop door was open, a couple of cars were inside but it was quite a mess. It was as though the last few people alive had desperately tried to get away from there to; somewhere; anywhere.

They finished their tour of the village and worked their way back to Liz's house, calling at a small corner shop which was much the same as the other shop but smaller. They had a look through the window, but as it was locked up, decided to leave that one for another day.

"Let's have some lunch, Mum," said Jane, "I'm hungry."

"That's the general idea girls, let's go home."

Meanwhile, the men had arrived at the police station to find Jack already outside having a look round. Ted, who had left Norman and Tony round the corner just out of sight, greeted Jack with a welcome handshake.

"Where are the rest?" Ted asked.

"They've been and had a look but had to go and try to find some dark glasses, it's a bit bright at first isn't it?" Jack replied.

"It certainly is for an hour or so, but there's something I've got to tell you. The friends I had with me yesterday."

"Oh yes," said Jack, "where are they?"

"They're just round the corner, and they're mutants, so I said I would tell you about them first to prepare you."

"What kind of mutants?" Jack asked cautiously.

"Well, you won't believe me until you've seen for yourself, but they're half horses."

"You're having me on," said Jack.

"No I'm not, but they're alright, come on Norman." Shouted Ted.

A couple of the others had appeared by this time but stayed behind Jack when Norman and Tony came round the corner.

Ted stood up to his full height of about five feet ten, stuck his chest out and said; "Jack, I'd like you to meet Norman Johnson and his son Tony, and Norman, this is police sergeant Jack Bright."

As a police officer for many years, Jack had experienced lots of strange things in his life, but this beat the lot, he couldn't believe his eyes.

"Pleased to meet you Norman," he said hesitantly, shaking his hand, then to Tony. "Forgive me if I seem a bit unsure of myself but I think you two are going to take a bit of getting used to."

"Make that four," said Norman with a grin, "I have a wife and daughter at home."

"Really, I just don't know what to say, but if Ted says you're alright then that'll do for me."

"Well, you'd better meet the rest, come on your lot and meet someone with a difference." And Jack introduced Norman to the rest of the group who had made up the syndicate. Jack's wife Wendy and their two children, who were now grown up, Rebecca twenty-four, and Steven twenty-two. Then there were four other couples making up the group, with five children between them.

"I bet you didn't recognise these two Ted, did you," pointing to Steven and Rebecca, "they were at school last time you saw them."

"I think I would have guessed if you hadn't told me, from how I remember them and they look like you two anyway."

With the introductions completed and a few cautious handshakes, the talk was what to do next. Ted went on to tell Jack about Jim and his family, then about Norman finding the

Websters, who Jack did remember because Harry Webster had been the manager of the bank that Ted used.

Jack, being a police sergeant, and one of the old school, soon made it clear that he was taking charge and wanted to be kept up to date with anything and everything that happened or was discovered, or more survivors found. Everyone agreed without question because the prospect of what was to come was daunting to say the least. Looking for anyone else alive was the first priority, and without her knowing it, Margaret Webster, being a doctor, was delegated as one of the search parties to check over any survivors that they may find.

Sgt. Jack Bright was not only a dedicated police officer but a thoughtful and caring man who had kept five families alive and sane in a confined space for a very long time. This helped him to keep his strict authority on the situation, his size also helped, six foot three.

So the chatting went on for an hour or so, the other families getting to know the Centaur's way of life and vice versa. While Ted and Jack, in between reminiscing, talked about the future and what would be the best method of approaching all the problems that they would undoubtedly come across.

For the rest of today, they all agreed that they would go and have a look at what was left of their homes. So Sgt. Bright made sure that everyone had a solar-powered intercom to keep in touch in case of any problems. (Crafty Jack had managed to acquire a box of new ones before the trouble started.)

So off they went, Jack, Wendy, Steven and Rebecca in the direction of their house and the rest of them split up to find their own homes. Ted had agreed to stay at the police station with Norman, Tony and Peter to keep an eye out and have a brief look round the immediate area, making sure radio contact was maintained at all times.

An hour later Ted was just about to start calling everyone up when the radio crackled into life, "Jack to base, you there Ted?"

"Yes Jack I was just about to start calling everyone up, anything wrong?"

"No, on the contrary you wouldn't believe it but our house looks just as we left it, not one window broken. But I'll not waste radio time I'll tell you when we get back."

Ted called the other four families and all reported back with no problems although there was mixed reaction to what they had found. Meanwhile, Norman and Tony had been having a look round the area not too far from the police station and realising that life in a town was not going to be easy for them. They couldn't get into shops without a lot of difficulty; they would never be able to have a car. It was beginning to sink in that although they were getting on well with the humans their life was going to be completely different. It hadn't seemed too bad at first, on the farm meeting Ted, then the Websters and dining together in the country. But town life was something else. Something they did find was a large area of land which had no buildings on it, but among all the undergrowth they found quite a variety of plants which looked like they might be good to eat. They had discovered a garden allotment plot where the town folk had still liked to grow their own vegetables. Quite a lot of what they found was the same as what they grew in their own garden, but they gathered one or two interesting plants to show Ted and try to establish if they were edible or not. They got back to the police station to find Ted on the radio to his wife Liz who assured him they were all fine and had had a very interesting morning in the village. Norman had a quick word with Mary telling her a bit about the town and reassured her they would not be too late home as they were beginning to feel a bit hungry.

Norman asked Ted if he wanted to have a quick look round while they were waiting for the others to return and suggested that he and Tony would man the radio, to which Ted agreed. The police station had extra-large doors, so even Norman could get in without too much trouble.

"Jack to base, come in Ted."

"Hi Jack, it's Norman, Ted's gone for a quick look round as we've just come back from having a walk ourselves. Everything's alright here, are you?"

"Yes, Norman, no problems. Just wanted to tell you we are on our way back, and can you call the others back in then we'll have time to pool our findings before you set off home."

"OK Jack, I'll do that, see you in a bit."

"Base to one, two, three and four, will you all start making your way back to base now please? Jack wants to collect all your information before we go so we can decide on tomorrow. Reply number one;"

"Yes, we were just setting off anyway."

"Reply number two;"

"Two to base, on our way."

"Reply number three," or "Reply number four, have you seen anything of three?"

"Four to base, no we've not seen them since we split up at their road end but it's only up the next street so we'll go have a look."

"Alright but be careful, any problems call in."

"Tony, go and find Ted, he only went round that first corner so he'll not be far away."

Tony set off at a gallop to find Ted; he would know what to do because this was all very new to the Johnsons.

"Four to base."

"Yes four, go ahead." replied Norman.

"We haven't reached them yet but we can hear a lot of shouting. We're nearly there. Hell's bells, what's that? It's like a woolly pig with horns and it's got them cornered in the garage."

"Hello four, don't go near it, climb up onto something."

"OK Norman, the reason they didn't reply is they've dropped their radio and can't get near it for this animal."

"OK four, make sure that your family is safe then find something to climb on as near to them as you can get in safety then try to distract it away from them so they can close the door or get themselves to a safe place."

"Right Norman, by the way I'm Colin."

In the meantime, Tony came trotting back with Ted, "What's up Norman." he puffed. Norman explained the situation and asked how far away Jack was as he remembered that Jack had his police pistol with him.

"I'm not sure," said Ted, "but I'll soon find out."

"Base to Jack, base to Jack."

"Jack to base, what's up Ted?" Ted explained the situation and discovered that Jack was about a mile away.

"OK Ted I'm on my way," said Jack, "should be there in about ten minutes. Jack had made a note of where everybody had gone so he knew where to go. At the same time, Ted had given directions to Norman on how to get there because he had encountered these creatures before and knew how to deal with them. Jack told Steven to get his mother and sister back to the police station as quickly as possible without running and tiring themselves out because although they had done some training in the shelter they were still not very fit."

"Ted to Colin."

"Yes Ted, go ahead."

"What's the situation?"

"Much the same, it won't leave them alone, it's not a bit interesting to me at all but Ken's managed to get his wife and daughter up on a shelf out of the way and he's holding it off with a wheelbarrow and a garden fork."

"OK Colin, help's on the way so try and shout and tell Ken to hang on for another few minutes, Jack's coming, he's got his handgun and Norman's coming from here, he's encountered these things before."

Ted's directions were spot on for Norman; as he slowed down from a gallop to turn the corner he could already hear the commotion, lots of shouting and banging. When he approached the creature, it saw him coming and turned to attack but Norman was ready for it and turned round and met it frill in the face with a pair of hind hooves. That slowed it down a bit but these things, which Tony had named Shigs, are extremely tough and very reluctant to give in. The males, which this one was, are much more aggressive than the females and he turned to have another go at Norman but once again was met with his lightning hoofs knocking it halfway across the road. But again it got up, raised its head into the air and let out an almighty bellowing scream, like a cross between a sheep's bleat and a pig's squeal but twice the volume. Ken had been watching from the garage and having a bit of a breather but he realised now that this thing meant business this time. As it started to run at Norman, Ken started to run at it with the wheelbarrow. Now it was undecided who to go for, Ken being the smaller looked the better bet and it turned on him giving Norman the chance to take advantage of the distraction and deliver another powerful back kick. It had picked itself up again and was just preparing for its next attack when Jack came puffing and panting round the corner. The shig hadn't heard Jack coming and Colin being nearest put his finger to his lips telling Jack to approach quietly. Norman realised that the shig had had a bit of a fight knocked out of it so this time he turned on it and delivered another almighty kick knocking it into a garden wall. This was the opportunity that Jack needed and while it was on the floor he was able to get a shot in its head, and even then it needed another one to kill it.

The Shig gets a kick from Norman's lightning hooves

"Thank God that's over," said Ken, "I thought it was going to have us for dinner, and thank you, Norman. I think you have just proved that you are going to be a useful mate to have around."

"Pleased to have been able to help, but I think it proves that it's a good idea to carry a gun, for the time being anyway," Jack agreed, but pointed out that there would have to be regulations and restrictions on usage as ammunition was limited until they could find some more.

They were preparing to set off when Norman said, "You're not leaving that behind, are you?"

"What?" said Jack.

"The shig," said Norman, "they're excellent meat and plenty of it."

"Hadn't thought of that," said Jack.

"Lay it across my back and I'll carry it back for you," said Norman, and they set off back to the police station.

The others had all got back safely when they arrived and were a bit surprised to see Norman carrying the dead animal on his back.

"Look what we've got for dinner," said Jack on approaching the waiting group. "Norman says they are good meat, so there you are, Eric, you're the butcher."

"You'll enjoy that," said Ted, "I know because I've already tried it, and Liz will have ours ready when we get home."

So they all swapped stories about how they had found their homes and what thoughts they had about the immediate future, with Jack taking notes of all the relevant important items. Then it was time for Ted, Norman, Tony, and Peter to head back home. But first, Ted remembered they had to check the radio frequency, as they had not been able to contact Jack before. "Of course, I'm still on the old police frequency," said Jack.

Having got that sorted out, the three set off, leaving the syndicate group licking their lips in anticipation of shig steaks. "I'll call you tomorrow, Jack," said Ted as they left.

Ted's son Peter was fairly quiet on the way home, riding in Norman's cart with his dad.

"What's up, Pete?" said Ted.

"Nothing," said Peter, "but I wish I could have seen that animal and Norman fighting."

"Don't worry, Pete," said Tony, who was trotting alongside the cart, "if you ever do see one in a bad mood you want to make sure you're up a tree, they're not nice to know." Peter had just felt a bit left out when the emergency had cropped up and he just had to keep out of the way.

"Never mind, son, we're going to the yard tomorrow, that should be a bit more interesting for you. I'm going to try and get that diesel generator checked over and see if it will ever go again."

"Will it be alright if we come too?" said Norman. "I can bring the cart again, you might need some things moving, and I would like to have a look in that timber yard we saw on the way into town."

"Sure, that would be great, save us walking."

Beth saw them coming in the distance and came trotting to meet them.

"Hi, Dad," she said, "Mum was getting a bit worried but dinner is only just ready anyway, Tony's so-called 'shig stew' and the vegetables we brought with us."

With the ladies very pleased to see the menfolk home again safely, dinner was enjoyed by everyone, not least the Pearsons, tucking into Norman's fresh veg.

"Right then, Ted," said Norman, "it's nearly dark, we must be going. I'll leave the cart here tonight and see you in the morning." Goodnights all round and the Johnsons set off back to the farm.

Mary and Beth were staying at the Pearsons' again while the men went to town.

"Make sure you're never too far away from your shotgun," said Ted to Liz as he was preparing to leave. "You know, just in case."

Liz had her own gun, as she had been a keen clay shooter, so she knew how to handle one. "Don't worry, love," she said, and joked, "you know I'm a better shot than you."

Norman had already hitched up the cart with a harness he had adapted from some he'd found in the old Johnsons' stable.

"Ready when you are, Ted," he said, "you too, Pete, jump in."

"Come on, Dad, let's go, I've been ready for ages," said Tony, "bye, Beth, bye, Mum."

"Should be a bit earlier tonight," said Norman as they left.

Once again, as they approached the town, Ted went extremely quiet.

"Stop here a minute, Norman, will you?" he said as they were crossing the motorway flyover. "It's eerie, I'm used to seeing lots of traffic moving up and down, but now look at it."

Norman had never seen it any different, except on video films. But now there was nothing moving, just a few vehicles here and there, some parked neatly, some in the ditch, and one looked as if it had just run into the back of another one.

"Right, Norman, let's go, but it does make me wonder if we really are the lucky ones, why are we here, what's our purpose, our future?"

"I don't know, Ted, but our parents, the Johnsons, they taught us about God and how we should be happy that we have been chosen to survive. They also said that any other survivors we may meet will have been chosen for a reason."

"You're probably right, but if the rest of the world is like this, we have a hell of a cleaning-up job ahead of us."

When they arrived at the yard, Ted jumped out of the cart. "Somebody's been here," he said, "pass me the gun, Pete."

"Careful, Ted," said Norman, "they're still here."

As they got near the workshop, they could hear somebody inside. Norman stood by the door with his gun ready.

"Come on out with your hands up, we've all got guns," he shouted, not thinking that there may be a few of them, but there weren't.

"It's alright, Ted, it's me," Jim had recognized Ted's voice.

"What are you doing here?" asked Ted. Jim was a bit surprised at Ted's slightly sharp question.

"I've come for my toolbox, I have my small one at home, but I remembered my other big one had been left here so I came to get it, do you mind?"

"Er, oh, no, of course not, Jim, sorry mate, it's just that this is taking a bit of getting used to."

"Anyway, how are you going to get it home?" Jim just grinned and said, "Come and look at this, I've come on my bike." He'd managed to get the tyres blown up with a little assistance from the garage which 'supplied' him with a new tube.

"That still doesn't tell me how you are going to get your toolbox home," said Ted.

"Turn around and look at this then," Jim showed him what he had been busy with. He had got the two-wheeled barrow that had been used for the gas bottles which was on solid rubber wheels, bent a piece of iron bar into an 'S' shape with a ring on one end, clamped it to the barrow, and he had a trailer for his bike.

"Now I know why I employed you," said Ted.

Jim's trailer invention wouldn't go through the side door, and the big up-and-over workshop door didn't want to open.

"I can see what's wrong," said Ted, "there's a bird's nest jammed in the top chain pulley."

"I'll get the ladder, it's still on the wall where we left it," said Jim.

So with the bird's nest dealt with and the help of a drop of oil, Jim soon had the door opening with ease.

Ted told Jim about meeting Jack Bright the police sergeant and the rest of the syndicate, and about the encounter with the 'shig'.

"That is a creature you don't want to tangle with," said Norman. And Jim pointed to his shotgun propped up against the wall.

"Well, it might just slow it down a bit," said Norman with a grin, "but be careful." And Jim was on his way.

So Ted set about checking all his tools and machinery and explaining to Norman what different things were for. Because although Norman was used to using most hand tools, he'd not seen things like this before.

Meanwhile, Tony and Pete were busy examining the old diesel generator that Ted was hoping to get going again.

"Do you think it will run again, Dad?" said Pete.

"Don't know yet, but I'll have a look in a minute."

Both Pete and Tony had been reading books on cars and mechanics and were keen to try the old engine. Pete picked up a starting handle from under the engine and slipped it onto the front of the crank.

"I think it's seized up, Dad, it won't turn over."

"It'll take more than you to turn that thing, son, hang on, I'll be there in a minute."

But they were just a bit impatient, like most lads, and carried on cleaning it; the tank was even still half full of diesel.

"Right then, lads, let's have a look at it," said Ted. He reached over and turned a small handle on the top of the engine.

"That's the decompression lever, it makes it easier to turn the engine over," Ted explained to them. Then it was his turn to have a go at the starting handle.

"Amazing," he said as the old engine started turning, "it's as though it was only run yesterday, but we'd better just check the fuel line and flush it through." Fuel line checked, he clicked the decompression lever back to see if it actually had any compression and it seemed to be good. Finally, he pulled out the dipstick to check the oil which was quite clean because the engine had never done a lot of work anyway, he only kept it as a standby. But it had belonged to his father and he wouldn't part with it. He screwed a new oil filter on which he had found on the shelf, just where he knew they would be.

Norman had been watching with interest, "What now Ted?" he asked.

"Let's see if she's going to go." He answered. It was a job he could normally do on his own but because it had been standing for so long he decided to have a bit of assistance.

"Right, Pete, open that lever again so I can turn it, then when I tell you, close it again."

The old engine started turning, slowly at first. Then Ted picked up speed.

"Now," he said, and Pete flipped the lever over. Ted managed three more turns and stopped.

"I thought I was being a bit too optimistic," he puffed, "but that should have got the fuel to the top. Now, this time."

Ted turned the engine furiously.

"Now," he shouted, and Pete once again flipped the lever over. With a big belch of black smoke from the exhaust pipe, it barked into life.

Only the slightest rattle for a split second, and then the oil was circulating fully, and the old engine was running as good as new.

"Would you believe it?" said Ted. "My dad always said it would never let me down." He stood looking at it lovingly. Then, wondering if the generator was working, he said, "Pete, will you get me an electric drill from that cupboard, please, and we'll try it." Ted had had a good look round his workshop, and nearly everything was exactly where he had left it.

"The voltmeter shows power, so here goes." He plugged it in, switched on, and the drill worked perfectly.

"Amazing," he said, "it's like we've never been away."

Norman and Tony had been standing back, watching with great interest when the old engine fired up. But now it was making electricity, Norman moved in for a closer look.

"Mr. Johnson told us about internal combustion engines and that some of them were used for generating electricity," said Norman. "We shall have to try and find one. What do you think, Ted?"

"Well, until somebody turns up to tell us differently, it looks like the whole world is ours for the taking at the moment."

"Can we really have one, Dad?" said Tony. "Well, Ted's the engineer so we'll leave it up to him at the moment and see what he comes up with."

Ted told them that the industrial suppliers that he had used occupied a very large warehouse and usually had a good stock of everything in. "It's not too far from here, just on the other side of the estate. And I've been thinking I could do with a small one for home anyway, we'll have a look before we go home."

Ted tried a few more of his tools and explained a bit more about his trade to Norman while the boys explored outside. Their next project was to see the truck running again, and the mobile crane. But that wouldn't be for a while yet.

Lunchtime was coming up so they decided what to do at the workshop for today. "Tell you what," said Ted, "do you want to see about a generator now, Norman?"

"Yes if you like, Ted, and if there's any more I can drop yours off at home for you," he replied.

"Great," said Ted, "let's go."

At the warehouse, the yard gates were wide open, a couple of trucks stood in the yard, but all the warehouse doors were closed except for a small side door.

"Hold it, Ted," Norman sensed something.

"What is it?" said Ted.

"I'm not sure," said Norman, "but something or somebody has been, and I think they're still here."

Ted pulled out his handgun, and Norman reached round and got his shotgun from the cart.

"Here, Tony, unhitch the cart while I keep an eye on Ted," he said, "then keep back and take care of Pete."

Tony unhitched the cart from his dad and stepped back to where Pete was.

"If it's a shig, jump on my back," Tony told Pete, "but somehow I don't think it is."

Ted crept up to the open personnel door with Norman right behind him.

"See anything, Ted?" Norman asked quietly.

"No, not yet, I'm going in."

Norman followed him.

"Slowly, Ted," another three or four paces, "stand still, Ted," Norman whispered, "it's behind those crates over there, you go that way, I'll watch this side."

Ted moved slowly along the row of boxes until just as he reached the end; out it came. It came round Ted's end of the crates and went straight for him. It appeared so suddenly it took Ted by surprise, he tripped over a pile of rubbish, fell over, and dropped his gun.

The 'thing' was about the size and shape of a man, maybe an inch or two taller than Ted. But it was wearing a hood and was covered in a large cloak and baggy trousers. Norman raised his gun to shoot, but it didn't bother with Ted at all, just jumped over him and came towards Norman. It was heading for the side door, but by this time Tony had appeared in the doorway, blocking it. The thing saw this and changed direction in a flash, and like lightning was behind some more crates.

"You alright, Ted?" Norman asked.

"Yes, I'm OK, but I feel a bit stupid, I could have been killed," Ted said.

"Maybe," said Norman, "but I don't think it wants to hurt us, it was trying to get out, stay there a minute." Ted stood where he was as Norman walked slowly to where the thing had gone.

"Hello," he shouted, "don't be afraid, we won't hurt you, we could have shot you, but we didn't." Norman moved a bit closer to the second row of crates where he knew the thing was hiding.

"Come on out and meet us, if you have a problem maybe we can help you." Then in a very high-pitched voice, almost a loud squeak, the thing answered. "No, I can't."

Norman moved round the end of the crates; the thing saw him and fled, along the aisle of crates to the loading bay. There it grabbed the chain for the up-and-over door, pulled until there was a gap at the bottom, rolled out underneath it, and was gone. Tony and Pete just had time to turn around and see it running out of the yard at a tremendous speed.

"It's gone, Dad," Tony said as the two men emerged from the building. "And it can't half run," said Pete.

"Well, it can speak, so it must be human of some kind," said Norman. "We shall have to mention it to Jack and see if we can catch up with it, or them, some other time," said Ted, "now, let's find some generators."

The Catman runs away

Ted had a good idea where they were.

"Hey, look at this, they must have known we were coming," he laughed. There was a stack of ten crates all with new generators in them.

"Here you are," he said, passing one to Norman, "they're not very heavy."

"Tell you what," said Norman, "we'll drop one off for Jim on the way back, we nearly passed his place anyway."

"Good idea," said Ted, "can you two lads carry one between you? We'll call back at my place and pick up some drums of diesel and try Jim and his wife for a spot of lunch."

So with the cart loaded up with three generators and six drums of diesel, they arrived at Jim's.

"Who do you think you are, Father Christmas?" Jim joked to Norman when they showed him what they had brought.

"No, on second thoughts, you're an angel, whoever invented you did a damn good job. What's for lunch, Jean? These lads have earned it."

Jean soon had the table on the lawn full of cold meat and salad, while the men told Jim about the creature they had seen in the warehouse.

"Now you come to mention it, have a look at these footprints in the garden." The footprints looked like rather large animals, but long like humans.

"I thought of monkeys," said Jim, "but the other day I thought I saw something out here, a man, when I got here it had gone but as I looked over the hedge there was something running away in the distance. The only other thing I found was a lot of feathers over there, probably caught a bird and eaten it."

"Sounds like the same fellow," said Ted, "but we don't think it's dangerous, just shy. What do you think, Norman?"

"Er, oh, yes I don't think they will bother anyone," Norman replied, deep in thought.

"Are you thinking what I'm thinking, Dad?" said Tony.

"I guess so," replied Norman, "but I'm sure there is nothing to worry about."

"You two have lost me now," said Ted, "let's eat."

"Thanks for a great lunch, Jean," said Norman, "but we've got to be going."

Jim's little lad Mike overheard.

"Oh, no, can't you stay a bit longer?" He had been having a great time riding round the lawn on Tony's back.

"Sorry, Mike," Tony said, "but we do have a really long way to go, but we'll come and see you again, and maybe you could come and stay at our farm sometime."

"Oh, great," said Mike, "can I, Dad, can I?"

"We'll see," said Jim.

The generators worked perfectly, and after the novelty had worn off, fuel conservation had to be a very important factor. Ted's main tank had about two thousand litres left in, but that wouldn't last forever.

So the days went by with Norman, between helping Ted to move a few things about, and was busy converting one of the better farm buildings into their new home. He had chosen this as a better option to start from scratch. Ted and Jim, however, were spending a lot of time together at Ted's yard.

"I think it's a must to get the truck going, Jim, don't you?" Ted was itching to be on the move properly. But there was quite a bit to do first, two flat tyres for a start, the brakes would all be well and truly stuck on. They had tried to make something of his old pickup truck but it was too far gone.

"Tell you what, Ted," Jim said, "remember Smithsons builders, they had just bought a new diesel pickup before we took them to the shelters, I wonder what it's like."

"That's an idea," said Ted, "let's go have a look." It was only about a ten minute walk.

The builders yard was, like everywhere else, deserted, but there was no sign of the pickup.

"Might be in the shed," said Jim, "I'll have a look." The shed was locked.

"Can't get in, and there's no windows," Jim reported.

"I'll try the office, there might be some keys in there," said Ted. The office was locked.

"We're not having a lot of luck here, are we?" Jim looked through the window, "Look there on the wall, keys, it's a pity but we'll have to break the window."

Jim picked up a brick from just near the office door and was about to break the window with it.

"Hang on, Jim, what's this?" said Ted, "Don't tell me, it's a key."

Said Jim, "Got it in one," said Ted, "but it's not for the office, it's the wrong type, but it could be for the shed." It was a brass key so it hadn't rusted away and with just a little bit of cleaning opened the shed door where sat looking at them was a quite reasonable looking pickup truck.

"Well, just look at that," said Jim, "and the tires are still blown up, amazing."

"I bet the battery's flat though," joked Ted.

"Tell you what we'll do, Jim," Ted said, "I'll give Norman a call when I get home and see what he's doing tomorrow. If he's available I'll get him to bring his cart and we'll go round to Central Motors and get some new batteries. They should still be alright because they haven't been used and they are all sealed anyway."

"Yes, good idea, charge 'em up at the workshop and we're away."

"You've got it, Jim, so in the morning you make a start on the truck's brakes and, assuming Norman's coming, we'll get some batteries sorted out for the truck and the pickup."

As Ted was locking the shed up again, Jim said, "Why are you locking it up? Nobody's going to steal it." Ted just grinned, "You never know."

Norman was at Ted's house early next morning, Tony had decided to stay at home with Mum and Beth, he wanted to get on with some work on their new home conversion, his room. But Liz and her two children were going to town with the men and were going to stay with Jim's wife, Jean, they knew each other before.

They all climbed in the cart.

"Everybody in," Norman asked.

"Ready when you are," replied Ted.

"Right, Jim's next stop."

Jane was quite excited about the cart ride because she had missed out when Pete had been to town before, and she was going to meet some more new people. So Pete was giving her a sort of running commentary on the way, pointing out things he had seen on his previous visits.

Jim was in the garden when they got there. "Morning, everybody," he shouted.

They all jumped out of the cart as little Mike came running up to meet them.

"Where's Tony?" he asked immediately.

"Tony's stayed at home today to do some work on our new house, but he'll come another day," Norman explained.

"Oh, I wanted Tony to come," he said disappointedly.

"Never mind," said Pete, "I'm not going with Dad today so we can have some fun here, can't we."

"Shall we go then," said Ted, "we've a lot to do."

"Can't wait," said Jim, "I get to ride there today."

As they were passing a timber yard Norman was having a good look over the fence.

"I'd like to have a look round there sometime," he said, "and get some timber sorted out for my place."

"No problem," said Ted, "we'll knock off early and call on the way back."

At Ted's yard all was well, just as they had left it. Ted and Jim jumped out of the cart.

"What's first," said Norman, "shall I drop the cart?"

"No, while you've got it on, we'll go and get some batteries. I know what we want for the pickup because I had a look yesterday but I'll just check which type they are for the truck."

"You alright with the truck brakes then, Jim?"

"Yes, no problem."

"Right then, Norman, we'll go get some batteries."

Central Motors had a real surprise waiting for them. In the showroom, behind the big plate glass window stood two 'new' pickup trucks.

"Look at them," said Ted, "it must be Christmas."

"They're not going to be much use to me though, Ted," Norman said with a chuckle.

"Er, no, course not, mate," Ted said apologetically, "but I bet Jack would like one. I'll not say anything, but if I can get them going I'll take him one tomorrow."

The door to the store was closed but not locked.

"You can stay here if you like, Norman. The batteries were just round behind this door. Let's hope there's some still here."

Ted emerged a couple of minutes later carrying a rather large battery still wrapped in polythene.

"Another one of these for the truck and we'll take three for the pickups and that'll do for today," said Ted, and loaded them onto Norman's cart.

Back at Ted's yard, Jim had already got the truck jacked up and the wheels off.

"Good man, Jim," said Ted, "any problems?"

"Not at the moment. In fact, they're in good condition considering the length of time they've been standing," replied Jim. "Anyway, I might have a surprise for you later," said Ted.

"What's that?" asked Jim.

"Wages," said Ted.

"You're joking," replied Jim, "what good's wages, where can I spend it?"

"Who mentioned money?" said Ted, "anyway, don't worry about it for now, we'll see later."

Norman had gone into the workshop with his cart and unhitched it.

"Where do you want the batteries, Ted?" he asked.

"Oh, near the generator, please. I'll bring the battery charger over. We'll charge two of the small ones first, then we can go and try the new pickups. The big ones for the truck can be on while we're away."

Ted cranked up the old diesel generator and plugged in the battery charger.

"Would you pass me those two leads off the bench, Norman? We'll put two on till lunchtime, that should do."

So they all worked on the truck until lunch, with Norman at the bench cleaning parts. He was really enjoying himself.

After lunch, Ted checked the batteries and they appeared to be OK.

"Why are you taking two?" asked Jim. He assumed they were going to Smithson's builders to get his pickup.

"Oh, er, in case one's no good," Ted replied. But they weren't going there; they were going to Central Motors.

About an hour later, Ted had one of the pickups purring like a kitten.

"I wonder if it's got any brakes," said Ted, and slid into the driver's seat. The handbrake had been left on and they were locked on solid.

"I thought it was going too well," said Ted. "Let's rock it backwards and forwards and see if that frees them." They tried and tried, but it was no good.

"Let's have a minute," said Ted, and leaned on the bonnet of the other pickup. It rolled backwards.

"I don't believe it," he said. Norman just laughed.

Norman had already fitted the other battery to the second pickup and primed the fuel line, and in about half an hour, it was also running.

"Let's take Jim his wages," said Ted, "and I'll come back tomorrow and sort the brakes out on the other one."

"I could have sworn Smithson's pickup was blue," said Jim when Ted pulled up in the yard.

"It is," said Ted, "this one's yours."

"What, where from?"

"Compliments of Central Motors," said Ted, "happy birthday."

"That's brilliant," said Jim, "thanks a lot, Ted, but what about you?"

"Well, there is another one up there, but I'll sort that out for Jack Bright, and I'll have the Smithson's."

Norman came trotting into the yard with his cart loaded up with a few more useful bits and pieces.

"We'll unload these bits, and then we'll be going, Jim," said Ted, "Norman wants to have a look round the timber yard on the way home. What time are you knocking off?"

"I shall only be about another hour. I'll get all the wheels back on, and that'll do for today," said Jim. "I can't wait to see Jean's face when she sees the pickup."

"Right," said Ted, "will you pick me up in the morning then, about nine?"

"No problem, see you in the morning."

Ted jumped in Norman's cart, and they left.

The timber merchant's yard was on the way back to Ted's house, but they had to go round by Jim's to pick up Liz and their two children. Norman had had a good look on the way past before, so he had an idea what he wanted. A lot of timber was stacked up outside, but some of it looked a bit rough. But the main shed offered a much better selection.

"What sizes do you need, Norman?" asked Ted.

"All sorts, really," Norman replied, "but hang on a minute, what's on this truck?" One of the company's trucks had been reversed into the shed and loaded ready for a delivery to somewhere. But it wouldn't be going anywhere else in a hurry.

"That truck could almost have been loaded for me," Norman said. "There's quite a lot of what I need on there, but it's too long for my cart."

"Well, don't worry about it for now, mate, I'll see if I can get something sorted out for you," Ted told him. "Anyway, we'd better get round to Jim's for Liz and the kids." They were all ready when the men arrived; the kids had heard them coming.

"Bye then, Jean," said Ted, "Jim won't be long, and he's got a surprise for you."

"What's that?" Jean asked.

"Won't be a surprise if I tell you, will it? Bye."

Then, with Ted, Liz, and the children in the cart, Norman headed for home.

They had all had an interesting day; although the women had been mainly sitting talking, there was a lot to catch up on. Pete wanted to know what had happened at the workshop and was really excited when his dad told him about the pickups.

Norman asked Ted if he needed a hand the following day, but he told him no as he had already been a great help and very much appreciated.

On arrival at Ted's house, everything looked normal.

"Everything's alright here, Ted," said Norman, "no problems."

"Thanks a lot, mate, I'll give you a call tomorrow night at about seven," Ted said, as Norman was leaving.

"OK, Ted, see you, bye."

Although Norman had decided to convert one of the old buildings, for obvious reasons, it would be only a single-story house. So, there was quite a bit of extension work going on to the ground floor. Norman had also made a ramp with an attachment to fit on one of the farm trailers; that was his form of scaffolding, or a working platform. It worked well because they could move it about wherever they wanted it. The original building floor was a good grade of concrete, as was some of the area outside the building. This is where he had extended the building to and was building on his extension.

But now he had just about used up all the timber that had been on the farm. He would have liked to have done some brickwork around the lower half of the wall, like he had seen in pictures, but not having any cement, that was impossible. Cement was something that they were going to have to do without for a long time yet.

Norman and Tony had finished breakfast early.

"I'll give Ted a call and see if he needs a hand; there's not much to do here today," he said to Mary. "Or is there something you wanted me to do?"

"No, not really," she replied, "in fact, Beth and I were thinking about going into the village to see Liz anyway."

"Right, I'll give Ted a call."

"Norman Johnson to Ted Pearson, you on air, Ted, come in." There was no reply. He tried again. "Norman Johnson to Ted Pearson, are you there, Ted, come in?" Nothing.

"They should still be switched on; it's only half past eight," said Mary. "I wonder if everything's alright." Everybody had agreed that they would all be switched on up to nine in the morning, and evenings from six until ten. "I'll try again, and then if there's no reply, we'll go over there anyway." He was just about to speak when:

"Hello, Norman, this is Liz, are you still there?" said the voice from the radio.

"Good morning, Liz," replied Norman, "is everything alright?"

"Yes, we're fine, did you want Ted?" she asked.

"Well, I just wanted to ask him if he needed a hand today as we've not much on," said Norman. "Oh, and Mary and Beth fancied coming over to your place for an hour or two."

"Well, Ted's already gone to pick Jim up," Liz replied. "He said they had a job to do for an hour or so, then they would call here and pick Jane and me up to come over to your place. I was just about to call you when you called me."

"That's great," said Norman, "we'll see you later then."

Norman had decided to do a bit of painting while Tony was perfecting his garden. They were both quite content doing their particular jobs when Tony trotted round to where his dad was painting.

"Can you hear that noise, dad?" he said.

"What noise?" Norman asked.

"It seems to be coming from the village, but I haven't heard it before," Tony replied.

"We'd better have a look then," said Norman, and they walked to the farm entrance where they could see down the road towards the village.

"There, Dad, look, a cloud of dust, looks like something just this side of the village," Tony was edgy. They watched for a while, then Norman said, "It looks like it's coming this way, go and tell your mum and Beth to get ready to go inside; I'll keep an eye on it." Norman watched as the dust cloud got closer; it turned at the junction and headed up the long straight road towards the farm. Norman stood his ground; only about half a mile away now. Then briefly the dust cleared, and Norman could see what it was. He trotted to the shelter.

"It's alright," he said, "come and have a look at this."

They all walked to the gate to meet Ted in his truck, with Jim, and Ted's family all squeezed into the cab. But, to Norman's delight, the truck was stacked high with the timber that he needed.

"Sorry about all the noise," said Ted, as they all climbed out of the cab, "but the old exhaust pipe fell off coming out of the timber yard."

"Another job for me tomorrow," Jim grinned.

"Thanks a million, Ted," said Norman, "You're a good mate."

"Well, we were going to tow the timber truck here as it was," said Ted, "but the front tire was flat and the brakes were stuck on as well, so we loaded it on mine. It's a good job there was room to get alongside."

"Well, once again, Ted, I just don't know how to thank you," said Norman, "but your timing isn't bad; Mary's just about got lunch ready."

"That'll do for us," said Ted, "we've worked up a bit of an appetite."

Over lunch, Ted explained to Tony about the exhaust pipe being noisy when there was no silencer fitted, and why it had been so dusty. The pipe had broken off just at a bend and left the remainder pointing at the floor.

"I was thinking about last week," said Norman, "the batteries at that garage, there should be one to fit Harry Webster's car, shouldn't there? I remembered it's a diesel, and he was tinkering with it when we were over at his place."

"Now that's a thought," replied Ted, "with Margaret being a doctor, it makes sense that she has transport, doesn't it? I'll give him a call tonight and check what type it is and see if I can get him one. You never know when we might need a doctor."

Ted delivers Norman's wood

"The Websters have been thinking of moving into the village," said Norman, "because although Margaret enjoyed the quiet life in the country before; she's a bit nervous out there on their own now."

"Well, there's a nice big house not far from us," said Ted, "used to belong to a solicitor, and it's in really good condition; we nearly moved in but Liz wanted our own."

"Anyway, Mary, thanks for lunch, that was great," said Ted, "come on lads, let's get this timber unloaded."

So the afternoon was spent with the ladies discussing whatever ladies discuss in the afternoon, and the men unloading the timber and stacking it under the open-sided shed.

Norman was delighted with his load of timber; he could get on with the roof now. As it was just a lean-to on the side of the original building, he had no problem reaching up to do the fixing; his trailer made an excellent working platform. He spent the rest of the week making fairly good progress, and Tony was getting more interested in the building of his new home.

Mary and Beth were also having their say in a few of the decisions and had quite an influence on the kitchen design.

Meanwhile, Ted had got Harry Webster fixed up with a battery for his car and got it going for him. He told the family about the big house in the village, and they decided to go and have a look round. Margaret quite liked the place, and Harry was equally happy to move into the village, as were the children. So Ted arranged a date with Harry and agreed to help him make the move with his truck. Caroline had been busy helping her mother with all the packing, while the twins, John and Carl, couldn't wait to see Ted's truck.

So the Websters moved into the village just round the corner from the Pearson's house. Harry had also been into town to meet Jack Bright, the police sergeant, and they had agreed that it would be a good idea to have a list of all the survivors, and hopefully add to it if they found anybody else alive. They would also log all the various different skills that everybody had and keep records of all the jobs that were done, and who did them.

Jack had the situation under complete control and had delegated Harry as his deputy, who was, as it happened, quite pleased to accept the job. Margaret, however, being the doctor, was in radio contact at all times and also volunteered to take on the job of school teacher. But they didn't intend to start school for a few weeks yet as there was too much work to be done first. Although there were eleven children at present between the ages of seven and twelve, plus Tony and Beth. Jack's twenty-four-year-old daughter, Rebecca, said she would help with the schooling of the younger ones.

But for the time being, everybody was fully occupied settling into their houses. The most important job was the servicing and fitting of solar panels for their power supply. Some were being transferred from the shelters, and others were obtained from houses that were known to have belonged to people who had perished. With Sgt. Bright's approval, of course.

Ted, being the engineer, was usually busy at his workshop making things or repairing them. But he wasn't content; he hadn't enough power to run his big machines and welding plants. He had been all over the place in his pickup truck, to all the other engineering places he knew, and their suppliers. But the only thing he had found that would do the job was an enormous static generator in the yard of what had been a plant hire company.

"That would do the job with no trouble," he said to Jim, "but how on earth can we get it back to the yard?"

"The mobile crane's the answer," replied Jim, "but that's not going to be usable for a good while yet."

"I know," said Ted, "but we've got to find some way of getting it onto the truck."

"How do you know it runs?" Jim asked casually.

"I don't," said Ted, "but we'll try it first before we go to a lot of trouble getting it home."

"Tell you what, Jim, would you like to get some batteries tomorrow and check it over, and I'll go and have a word with Norman and see if he has any ideas. I want to see how he's getting on with his house anyway."

"No problem," said Jim, "you know I like a challenge."

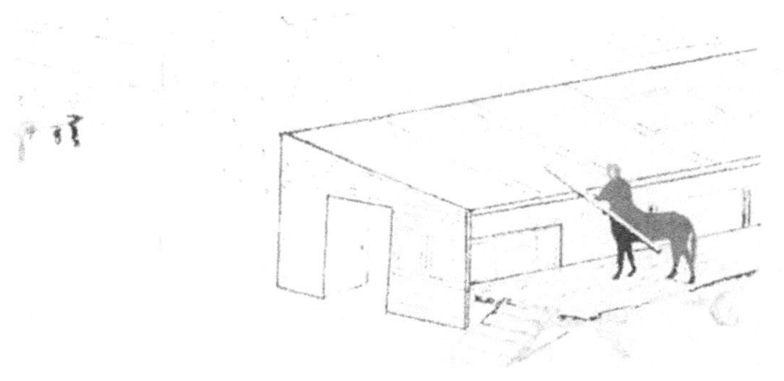

Norman works on his roof

The next day, Mary and Beth had been for a walk down the lane when Beth had spotted the dust rising over towards the village. "I'll go and tell Dad," she said and trotted back to the farm ahead of her mother.

"Dad, I think someone's coming," she shouted to him excitedly.

"OK, I'll come and have a look." Tony had heard his sister call and came round the end of the building from his garden. There was still a certain amount of tension when something different happened; even life itself in a basically human environment was never going to be easy for the Centaurs.

Ted pulled into the yard in his pickup truck to a cheery wave. "Hi, Ted, how are you?"

"Hello, everybody, I'm fine, how are you?" he replied.

"We're all well, thanks, how's Liz and the children?" Norman said, just as he noticed Pete sliding out of the passenger door.

"They're OK, especially now the Websters have moved in just round the corner," said Ted.

Pete went off with Tony to his garden while Norman took Ted round to show him how he was getting on with his new home. "Hey up, mate," Ted exclaimed, "you aren't half getting on with this, you'll soon be moving in."

"Oh, we'll be a while yet, and I was going to ask you if you would be able to give me a hand with the roof."

"No problem at all," Ted replied, "and actually, one of the reasons I'm here is to ask you a favour." Ted went on to tell him about the big generator and how he didn't know how he was going to get it to his yard.

"What's it like?" asked Norman. "And what's the ground like that it's stood on, is it level?" Ted explained that the yard was concrete and was split level at one end for loading machines onto trucks, but the generator was on the lower level.

"When do you want it?" Norman asked.

"Well, assuming it actually works, Jim's checking it over today, as soon as possible. Why, any ideas about getting it on my truck?" Ted queried.

"I don't think it'll be a big problem," said Norman, "just let me know when."

"Come on, then, mate, don't keep me in the dark, how are you going to do it?" quizzed Ted.

"You'll see," said Norman with a big grin, "just let me know when, and I shall need you to pick me up with your truck."

"Great," said Ted, "I'll give you a call tonight and let you know if Jim got it running."

Norman was quite interested in history and had read a lot of books on the subject. So Ted's problem had triggered his memory immediately, how the stone-age people had moved unbelievably heavy stones on wooden rollers. Round the back of the yard under another lean-to roof was a pile of wooden telegraph poles, and because they were always treated with preservative, they were still in good condition. Ted had given him the measurements of the generator, so the poles just needed cutting to length.

Old Mr. Johnson had used the poles for firewood before the war, and Norman remembered being told how they used to sit round a big log fire in the winter time. So this was one of the features that Norman was building into his new home, a big open fireplace. This could only be done by Norman's own version of dry stone building, not having any cement, but he was doing a fairly good job sealing it with clay which he was digging down by the stream.

That evening, after dinner: "Ted to Norman, you there, mate? Come in."

"Yes, Ted, go ahead," replied Norman.

"No problem with the generator," said Ted, "Jim says it sings like a bird, is tomorrow OK?"

"Sure, that'll be fine," said Norman, "It'll give me a break from this job, what time?"

"I'll be there about half past eight, that alright?" said Ted.

"Yes, I'll be ready, see you in the morning then, good night, Ted."

"Good night, Norman."

Ted pulled into Norman's yard in his truck at spot on eight thirty; Norman had heard him coming and was there to meet him.

"Morning, Norman," he said as he jumped out of the cab, "what's the mystery then, what are we taking with us?"

"Good morning, Ted," Norman replied, "bring your truck round to the back of that big shed and you'll see, there's plenty of room to turn round so you can drive in." Ted saw the poles that Norman had cut to length.

"Now why didn't I think of that," he said. "Probably because you still wouldn't have been able to move it anyway," Norman answered, "but me and Tony can, but we still may need your help. We will just have to call at your workshop and pick up two heavy-duty jacks."

"Norman, you're amazing," said Ted, "and are you two riding on the truck?"

"We certainly are," said Norman, "that's our ramp over there, we'll take it with us."

Jim fires up the big generator

Jim was at the yard waiting for them when they got there; Ted had intended going back to pick him up anyway. "Of course," he said when he saw the poles, "roll it on."

"You've got it, Jim," said Ted, "can you just get two big jacks, the red ones, then we're away."

In the plant hire compound, Norman and Tony jumped down off the truck and started unloading the poles, while Ted and Jim were busy jacking up the generator at one end. When it was high enough, Norman rolled a pole under the end, and the generator was lowered onto it. The other end had to be a bit higher so they could get three more poles under the whole frame and one more at the end. It was then lowered onto all the poles and ready to roll. Tony had a harness the same as the one Norman used for pulling the cart because he used it sometimes, so they put them on and tied ropes from them to the generator. Ted had already backed his truck up to the high level and was ready with Jim at the back of the generator.

"Right, Ted, you know what to do," said Norman, "when a pole comes out the back, put it back under the front. And will you keep one of those blocks with you to put behind the back pole when we need a breather, so it doesn't roll back down the slope."

Moving the big generator up the ramp

Norman and Tony started to pull, and it was going fairly easily to start with until they got going up the slope to the higher level.

"Can you give us push lads?" puffed Norman, "you'll have to block the next pole each time one comes out while you carry the free one to the front."

So between them they pulled the generator onto the truck. Once it was loaded, Ted secured it with chains and also nailed two blocks each side of the back and front pole to make sure it didn't roll off on the way.

Back at Ted's yard they hadn't really decided how they were going to get it off the truck. Jim came up with the answer.

"Roll it straight onto the old scrap trailer in the corner," he said, "and leave it on there, we'll just need a bit more cable."

"Yes, I think that will be OK," said Ted, "and it can stay there, for now anyway."

So Ted had his generator, although he didn't have a lot of use for the machinery it would drive, he was a man who liked to be fully equipped for any event.

"Right then Norman," Ted said, "once again many thanks, when you're ready I'll give you a ride back home in time for lunch."

Norman and Tony walked up their ramp onto the truck and pulled the ramp up after them. "Ready when you are Ted." Said Norman.

"Right, what about you Jim," said Ted, "are you having an early lunch?"

"No," replied Jim, "I'll just have a ride round to the warehouse and pick up some more cable first, then we might get the generator wired up this afternoon."

"OK Jim," said Ted, "see you later."

Ted had already passed his village on the way to Norman's farm when his radio crackled into life:

"Jim to Ted, Jim to Ted, come in Ted."

"Yes Jim, what's wrong?" Ted replied.

"Ted, I'm at the warehouse, there's been an accident, someone's trapped." Said Jim.

"Who's trapped, who's with you?" Ted asked.

"Nobody with me, when I got here there was someone in the warehouse, a man I think, and when he saw me he ran and knocked into some big crates and they fell on him. He's underneath and I can't lift them, I don't even know if he's still alive."

"OK Jim, we'll be there as soon as we can."

Ted had stopped his truck to listen to Jim and Norman had leaned over the front and been listening in to the conversation.

"I heard all that Ted," he said, "we're nearly at the farm now so if you turn round there I'll tell Mary what's happening and we'll come back with you."

"OK Norman, thanks, better call the doctor as well."

"Ted to Doctor Webster, you there Margaret, come in?"

"Yes Ted, I heard it all, I'm already on my way, I know the warehouse, I'll see you there."

Police sergeant Jack Bright had also heard Jim's call and was at the warehouse when Ted got there. Norman and Tony jumped down off the truck and hurried inside to see what had happened. Margaret was already there examining the only thing visible, a leg sticking out from under the crates.

"Are you sure this is a man Jim?" she asked, "This is an exceptionally hairy leg for a human."

"Well it looked like a man, maybe a couple of inches taller than me, but it had a hood on." Jim explained.

"It sounds like the same as what we saw before," said Ted, "but let's see if we can shift these crates."

"Hold it Ted," said Norman, "you'll not lift them, me and Tony will lift this one that's on him, then you slide him out, carefully."

The Centaurs took the strain and raised the crate enough so Ted and Jim could pull the 'man' out, Jack stood by with his hand gun at the ready, just in case.

What they pulled out was a bit of a surprise to them all. It looked like a man, in build anyway, but the head looked more like that of a cat, but human size.

"Just as I thought," said Norman, "I got a mental image of this the first time we saw him, when I heard his voice."

"You mean you knew what it was?" asked Jack.

"No, not really," said Norman, "I just had a vision of what it might be."

"Really." Was all that a surprised Jack could mutter. Anyway, whatever it was, it was unconscious.

Margaret checked it over as best she could, not knowing whether it was human or animal.

"A broken leg to start with," she said, "but I don't think there's much more."

Luckily one end of the crate had fallen on about half a dozen bricks and prevented the creature from being crushed completely. It started to regain consciousness, but as Margaret had given it a sedative injection, it was quite drowsy. The thing was terrified, tried to curl up in a ball, and tried to pull the hood back over its head. Margaret tried to console it.

"It's alright, we're friends, we want to help you, but don't try to move, your leg is broken." Norman moved in to speak.

"Are you the one that was here the last time?" The creature just nodded.

"Don't worry," said Norman, "we really are here to help you, and if you're bothered about being a mutant, you don't have to, look at me and my son."

"What are you going to do with me?" it was that squeaky voice again.

"Well we'll take you home for a start, and this lady is Doctor Webster, she'll make sure your leg gets better, where do you live?"

The creature went on, although drearily, to tell them that they had been born in an old underground mine out on the north side of the town where a number of couples had taken refuge when the war had started. There were two couples still alive but were not in a very good state, with bad skin burns, who had decided to stay in the mine, they just didn't have the energy left to try and go back to how it was before. The old people had called these creatures the 'Catfolk' and they were the descendants of a couple who had died some time ago. This one's name was Jan and he had a brother Tom and a sister Sue, and he being the eldest went out to look for food. The reason he had been on a couple of occasions was because when he was out at this side of the town he had stayed overnight in the warehouse.

Tony had found two pieces of wood to make splints for the catman's leg, and some clean cloth to pad it with. Margaret did the best she could under the circumstances; it wasn't a complicated break, it had just snapped sideways as the crate had fallen on it. So, with the help of Jack's first-aid knowledge, they strapped up Jan's leg.

It was decided that Jim would take him home in his pickup, Margaret would go with him to settle him down and reassure his brother and sister that he would be alright and also to have a look at the other people with the burns. Maybe she could do something to help them a little. Jack also said he would go along to have a look and try to reassure the old people that it wasn't the end of the world and not really too bad at all.

"Right then Norman and Tony," said Ted, "I'll take you two home again, and let's hope we get there this time."

Jim took it nice and steady through the town on the way to the old mine. Jan the catman had been made comfortable in the back on some thick cloth they had found in the warehouse, Margaret and Jack rode in the back with him. As they approached the mine, they saw two figures disappear at lightning speed into the mine entrance. The mine had a ground-level entrance dug into the hillside and one of the kinds that big dump trucks used to drive in and out of. But now the large opening had been bricked up, and only an ordinary personnel door was used. Jim pulled up outside and switched off the engine, Jack jumped out gun in hand.

"Just in case," he said, "can't be too careful." A man appeared at the door.

"Hello," Jack said, "it's all right, I'm a police officer, nothing to be afraid of."

"What's the gun for?" The man asked.

"Oh, it's just that there are some fairly dangerous mutant creatures wandering about, you know, just in case," Jack replied, putting his gun away.

"So who were those two who came running in here just as we were coming?" He continued.

Another face appeared at the door.

"That was Tom and Sue, why, you're not going to shoot them are you?" The first man said.

"No, of course not," said Jack, "in fact, why we're here is, we've brought their brother Jan back, he's had an accident, broken his leg."

Margaret had walked over by this time.

"And this is Doctor Webster," he continued, "Jan told us some of you had suffered some burns, she may be able to help you."

"I doubt it," said the man, "Tom, Sue, come on out, Jan's here, he's hurt."

Two furry faces appeared cautiously at the door; they'd never seen a vehicle before, and that's what had frightened them.

"Hello," said Margaret, "don't be afraid, we're here to help you."

Jim had been standing at the truck with Jan.

"Hello you two," he said as they nervously approached the pickup, "you must be Tom," to the larger of the two, "I'll give you a hand to get Jan inside."

Inside, Margaret made him as comfortable as possible and gave some pain-killing tablets to one of the older people.

"These are painkillers," she said, "only give him two if he needs them and no more than two every four hours, and I'll come back tomorrow and see how he is."

So that had been another eventful day. Jack arranged for Margaret to pick him up the next day so he could go with her. First of all, he wanted to make sure she was alright, and secondly, to have a good chat with the other people and bring them up to date with the rest of the survivors. Also, one of his main objectives was to get all the survivors to live not too far from each other, and try and build a fairly close-knit community. And that was to include the cat folk, and anyone else that may turn up with unusual appearances.

Norman spent a lot of his spare time studying agriculture, especially the farming of corn because all the people he had met had said they missed fresh bread. The Centaurs, however, had enjoyed fresh bread on very rare occasions.

The Johnsons' shelter was a large converted farm building, partly dug into the hillside. And as well as housing their animals, they had kept an area for growing vegetables, part of which had been used for growing wheat. Only about three square metres, but enough to produce enough corn to grind into flour and make a couple of loaves as a treat at Christmas. So Norman's time now was shared between working on his house and farming.

Mary was obviously quite impatient and wanted to be moving into the new house as soon as possible, but the land had to be worked at the right time. Norman had chosen a field that needed the least clearing and had started doing a lot of the work by hand, and Tony had also been helping as much as possible, but it was extremely hard work and was taking a long time to get a little bit done.

"I think I'll have a word with Ted," Norman said to Tony one day while they were digging.

"What about?" Tony asked.

"Well there's three tractors in the machine shed, and the implements don't look too bad, just a bit rusty," said Norman.

"How can we drive tractors?" Tony queried.

"We can't," replied Norman, "but one of Jack's men could, I think I'll call a meeting with Ted and Jack and see if we can get this farm running as it should be."

So a meeting was called for the following week at the farm and would be attended by Ted, Jack, Harry, Jim and two of the syndicate survivors.

The day of the meeting arrived and Ted had already been to see Norman and got one of the tractors running; he wanted to assure the meeting that what Norman had in mind was going to work. Jack arrived in his pickup with his two men and also Jim, as fuel had to be conserved as much as possible. Ted had picked up Harry so the car was available for Margaret if she needed it.

Norman assumed the position of chairman as he had decided on the meeting in the first place and he was, at this point anyway, the one with the most to say, and the meeting got underway.

The first item on the agenda was the need to start growing wheat as soon as possible, which was agreed by everyone. There was plenty of time to get the combine harvester working ready for when the time came to gather the crop.

"Where's the seed coming from?" asked Ken, one of Jack's men.

"Well we have a little," said Norman, "it's what we've grown in the shelter, we usually make some bread with most of it and just keep a bit for next year's seed, but this year we'll keep it all for seed as it's good quality."

He went on to tell them that he'd been all over the surrounding fields to see what was growing and had found one particular field to have quite a lot of wheat in it, probably the last crop that had been planted and been self-setting ever since. They had tried this wheat themselves and it was not too bad for bread making and would have to wait until they had enough of the good stuff to use. So, volunteers for gathering the wild wheat please, as it was harvest time about now they could all be having fresh bread before Christmas.

The next item was obviously how to grind the corn as Norman and Mary had been grinding theirs by hand.

"I think we can solve that problem fairly easily," said Jack, "there's an old nineteenth-century windmill not too far from here, it had been restored and was still in use so that shouldn't take a lot of cleaning up."

"I know the one," said Ted, "me and Jim can have a look at that one day and let you know what it's like."

Norman then went on to tell them that although he had a fully working tractor and all the implements to go with it, for obvious reasons he needed a driver. Jim volunteered without hesitation, he had always had connections with the land and had worked on a farm before working for Ted, and he loved tractors.

Ken and the other syndicate member Eric, volunteered to come up to the farm regularly to work in the fields and would travel with Jim in the other pickup he had rescued from the garage. They agreed to start the next day and get all the wild wheat in before it started falling on the ground.

The meeting went on until lunchtime when Mary had prepared a meal for everyone. The afternoon was spent walking round the fields and deciding what could be gathered and what was no good.

Apart from the wheat, there was a varied selection of strange vegetables, some of which very closely resembled what they were supposed to be. Some potatoes were excellent and there appeared to be enough to gather for eating now and plenty to keep for seed the following year.

"What about some sacks to put the corn in," asked Jim. "We can't handle it in bulk at the moment."

"I've been thinking about that," said Norman, "but all I can find is a few bundles of plastic sacks, and they've had fertiliser in so we can't use them."

"There should be some at the old mill," said Jack.

"Good thinking," said Ted, "we'll have a ride over tomorrow and have a look round, alright with you Jim."

"No problem," said Jim, "we can check the mill over at the same time."

"Well I think things are looking good," said Norman, "is everybody happy with what we've achieved today?"

"There's just one very important point we will have to do something about," said Ted, "fuel, we're going to have to find a supply of diesel from somewhere, my tank isn't going to last forever."

"I'll sort that out," said Jack, "I'll see who's available tomorrow and we'll have a ride out to the tanker depot and see what we can find."

The meeting had been a great success and life was beginning to return to some kind of normal, for the humans anyway.

Norman however was beginning to realise that although he was different, he and his family were fitting in with, and had been accepted by the humans one hundred percent.

He had been over to see the catfolk with Jack one day and suggested that they move into a smallholding between his farm and the village. The old couples said they had decided they would like to be nearer the rest of the community now they realised that there were other survivors. They liked the idea of living in the village, as it would not be too far from Doctor Webster. The catfolk were quite excited about the smallholding and couldn't wait to have a place of their own, but there would be a lot of cleaning up first as Norman had pointed out.

The next morning Ted arrived at the Johnson's farm with Jim, Ken and Eric.

"Morning Norman," said Ted, "I've brought you a couple of workers, Jim and me are going on to the mill, should be back by about mid-day."

"Ok Ted," shouted Mary from the other side of the door, "I get the message, lunch will be ready."

"Sorry if I sound a bit greedy Mary," replied Ted, "but you certainly do know how to feed people."

Ted and Jim left heading for the mill and hopefully returning with some sacks for the corn.

"Ready lads," said Norman, "Well concentrate on the potatoes this morning, I've got all the tools we'll need in my cart, you can ride if you want."

"How many are we getting, Dad," asked Tony, "are we digging them all?"

"No, we'll just pick the best from that one field, then it will be ready for Jim to plough when he gets organised with the tractor. Then the rest in the other field we can dig as we need them."

By late morning they had dug enough to last the whole community a week or two.

"We'd better get these loaded up or we'll be late for lunch," said Norman, "I'll hitch the cart up."

Ted and Jim were already back from the mill when they reached the farm.

"Been tatey pickin' lads?" Jim joked. "We've had a good morning as well, and brought half a dozen bundles of sacks back, I've put them in the tool shed."

"Thanks Jim," said Norman, "where's Ted?"

"He's already at the table," said Jim, "he really loves your wife's cooking."

The conversation over lunch was enthusiastic to say the least with everyone looking forward to the farm producing real fresh food at last.

"How's the mill then Ted," said Norman, "will it grind our corn?"

"Not at the moment," replied Ted, "but I think we can sort it out. Two of the sails are damaged, but I think if we can get them all balanced it will do for now."

"Ok then," said Norman, "we all might as well spend the afternoon gathering wheat now we have some sacks to put it in. What I had in mind was just clipping the ears off with shears or knives and filling the sacks so we don't have to carry too much straw home. I can gather enough straw for our animals as I need it."

By teatime Norman's cart was loaded with sacks of corn.

"That'll do for today," he said, "I think we should have it all in by next week. When we get back to the farm we'll fill three sacks with potatoes for you to take with you Jim, drop one off with Ted to share with the Websters, and take the other two for you and the others in town."

"I can't wait to have a pan of chips," said Ken, "how about you Eric, but what are we going to fry them in?" Eric just grinned and nodded knowingly. When he had butchered the shig and shared it out between the others, he had kept all the fat and rendered it down and ended up with a very large bowl of dripping.

"Tell you what Ken," said Eric, "just bring your wife and daughter round to our place for dinner tonight."

Meanwhile, Jack had enlisted Colin for the day, and they had been out to the tanker depot and discovered not one, but two road tankers full of diesel. He decided to let Ted know what he'd found.

"Jack Bright to Ted Pearson, you there Ted? Come in."

"Evening Jack, everything alright?" replied Ted.

"Yes, fine Ted, we found two tankers full of diesel, do you think you will be able to get them home?" Jack asked.

"More than likely, what are they, eight wheelers or articulated?" asked Ted.

"They're arctic, but they've got a couple of flat tires." Jack replied.

"No problem," said Ted, "all I have to do is release the brakes, pull the tractor unit out and couple mine up to bring them home. I'll take some spare wheels out in the pickup and get them both ready, then go out with the truck the next day. I could go tomorrow, are you available to come with me as back up?"

"Yes, I can be," said Jack, "pick me up in the morning."

"Ok then, see you Jack, good night."

"Night Ted."

So the future looked good for the Johnsons; the rest of the surviving community had accepted them one hundred percent. The catfolk had also been fully accepted as part of the community and were doing an excellent job of renovating the smallholding and growing a good selection of salad foods. Eric was kept busy nearly full-time as a butcher and hunted for his meat as was required. Meanwhile, Ted resumed his trade as an engineer, Jim worked with him part-time, and part-time with Norman in the fields, tractor driving. They had been to the old mill and put that back in commission, so after the harvest, they had plenty of wheat to grind for flour.

Ted had also been to the oil refinery tank depot and brought the two tankers full of diesel back to his yard, which he estimated would last them at least two years.

Jack maintained his authority as a policeman, but he didn't have much to do in that line of work, mostly just keeping a check on firearms and ammunition. He had been out to a gun shop that he remembered and returned with the full stock of shotgun cartridges and rounds for the six handguns he had issued to his men. He also brought four rifles and the ammunition to go with them; he considered they would be better for tackling the shigs. But his biggest concern was the burying of the dead, and he wanted to bury each family in their own garden where possible. So with the help of his son Steven and another of the men, they gradually gave each perished family their own funeral. This was initially to be only in the immediate area where they lived. On his rounds, he had found a mechanical digger which Ted had managed to get working again, so they didn't have a lot of digging to do. Harry Webster was also organising a similar operation in the village. Harry's wife Margaret, as well as being the doctor, had with the help of Jack's daughter Rebecca, got the school cleaned out and operating. They had decided on the village school so Margaret was not too far from her medical supplies if she needed them. It just meant she had to go into town each morning to pick up the other children.

Tony and Beth had their own desks built and joined in with the rest. Norman had enlarged one of the doors to the classroom, but apart from that, there were no problems. They were just two kids at school like the rest.

Norman had finished his new home and Mary had got it decorated just the way she wanted it. Liz Pearson had been giving her a lot of help with the interior as they had turned out to be the best of friends.

They now had a small but very active and efficient community all agreeing at this time, for safety reasons, to live fairly close to each other in the village just south of town, with Norman's farm not too far away.

Jack had also been responsible for persuading the rest of the syndicate to move into the village as he had done for obvious safety reasons. His house was quite big, so was also the police station.

They now had a school running, the village shop had been cleared out and anything of any use had been kept and for the time being Eric ran it as it had a big fridge for his meat.

Margaret had turned one of her rooms into a surgery, just in case there was a need. Norman was always busy on the farm and doing any joinery that was needed. Ted spent most of his time at his workshop, getting anything mechanical back into working condition again. He had also fixed everybody up with a portable generator for when they needed electricity and a bigger one for the shop.

Policeman Jack was in charge, which all agreed with, and the rest were all doing whatever they could.

It was autumn and although the weather was usually quite settled nowadays, they had to prepare for winter. They hadn't experienced cold weather for quite some time and the younger children hadn't ever seen snow or frost. There wasn't going to be much to do if the weather was really bad, so the library and book shops had been well sorted through for any good reading, toys, and games. The library had been especially useful for information on all the things they didn't know, like milling wheat into flour and making clothes, because although there were plenty of shops with lots of clothes still in good condition, they wouldn't last for ever.

George had volunteered to try and run the windmill when necessary as he was keen on rural history and had a bit of a head start. Ted had improvised on repairs to the mill because two of the sails were broken, but luckily, they were opposite each other so he removed the two broken ones to make a balance, it did work with a good wind, enough for what they wanted anyway until they could make some new ones. (A job for Norman!)

"Morning Norman," said jack as Norman opened the door for him. It was raining and not a good day for digging graves, even with a machine. "I've been thinking about the mill, do you think we could get the new sails made over the winter?"

"Don't see why not Jack," Norman answered. "When Ted took the old ones off to balance it he brought them back here for spares, but I could use one as a pattern to make new ones. There's plenty of room in the barn to lay them out and if Ted gets the crane working it won't be a big job to fit them." Ted had dismantled the broken sails on the mill and just let them fall on the floor, then with his mates lifted them onto his truck in bits. He had also, with the help of Jim, managed to tow the combine harvester into the barn with the tractor so he could work on it over the winter.

"Good morning, Jack," said Mary from the kitchen. "Would you like a drink?"

"Yes, please Mary, I'd like a coffee if you've got one going."

They had decided that although tea, coffee and sugar from the shops were well out of date, they were still drinkable, but always made sure the water was well boiled when brewing. As well as that they had also tried other foods that were in sealed packaging. Some biscuits were as good as new as were many tinned foods.

"Anyway Jack," said Norman. "I've been thinking about food for the winter, I've got all the potatoes in the shed over there, they should be enough for all of us. But just in case, I've planted a few more in the shelter where we grew them before and as you know, in there we can grow them any time. We can have new potatoes for Christmas."

"What a star," said Jack. "You really do think of everything, and Eric has made room in the shop for all the flour."

"Ted to Jack, you there, mate?" Jack's radio crackled into life. "Wendy said you'd gone over to Norman's, is everything OK?"

"Morning Ted, everything's fine, just discussing food for winter, what's up?"

"No problems Jack I just wanted a chat about those families who called themselves the 'hillsiders', can you call in on your way back?"

"Sure Ted, see you in about half an hour." So, Norman and Jack rounded off their chat, Jack thanked Mary for the coffee and set off back to the village.

Jack arrived at Ted's place to be greeted by Liz. "Good morning, Jack, he's just gone to his shed for a few minutes 'till you got here."

"Thanks Liz I'll see what he's up to"

"Morning Jack," Ted's voice came from the shed. "Come in."

"It's funny you should mention the hillside group, because I've been thinking about them as well," said Jack. "We know the Johnsons are somewhat telepathic, but I didn't think we were. Anyway, what were you thinking about?" Ted put his tools away. "Well, you have just been talking to Norman about the subject, the mill sails. When he's made them, my crane isn't big enough to reach, and in any case, it probably wouldn't travel that far anyway."

"Exactly," said Jack. "But we pass a big one regularly, Mark Blackwell's, it's a twenty-one-ton model and can reach over thirty metres with the extension on."

Mark was one of the hillside group, who had decided to get together and form a small community. There were four couples whose families had all grown up and left home to have their own families and lives. Some had emigrated and others moved away.

Mark had run a mobile crane business with his wife, Colleen.

Bill Major was an excellent machine shop engineer and wife Jenny ran a market garden. Paul Saunders had his own electrical business with wife Pauline and studied solar power. Wilf Williams had a very successful building company with wife, Claire.

They were all very smart people and when they got together, they decided to acquire a particular spot of land on a hillside about fifteen miles away. They knew if the worst happened money would be useless, so they pooled most of their assets and bought the land. Wilf, being the builder designed a super shelter and with the approval of the others, spent most of the remaining money building it. It was on a similar theme as a traditional row of terraced houses with initially one big shelter with three dividing walls making four homes. Within the shelter was a communal passage linking all four homes so they could visit each other if and when they chose to. With Paul's knowledge of solar power, they had plenty of facilities. Bill had designed and made a periscope so they could see what was going on outside. Mark, who was also a professional welder, had been on hand with his crane for all the lifting and any welding jobs. It had also been commented in the past that if anybody was going to survive, they would.

"Tell you what Jack," said Ted. "What about having a ride out there now, it's a rainy day and I'm not busy."

"Well, I suppose we could," said Jack. "I wanted to get out there before the bad weather anyway, we could be back by lunch time, unless they're all OK and invite us for lunch." Jack said with a grin.

"Jack to Norman, you there, pal?"

"Sure Jack," replied Norman. "What can I do for you?" "Ted and I are going out to where that hillside group went to live, do you remember I told you about four families who built a big communal shelter?"

"Yes, I remember, what do you want me to do?"

"Well, we're going over there and will be out of radio contact for quite a while, so can you keep your ears on for the rest of the village until we get back?"

"No problem, Jack, but be careful, you never know what might be out there."

"OK Norman, I've got my hand gun as you know and Ted's got his shotgun so we'll see you later."

Jack let all the others know where they were going, Harry and Ken both knew where the place was, so they would know where to look for them if necessary. They realised that they had taken a few risks in the past when wandering off alone, so now they didn't.

Ted drove steadily up the main road out of town past Norman's farm which was one field in from the main road. From there on they had not been any further until now. So it was exploration time once again. The road wasn't too bad but every now and then there would be an obstacle of some kind to negotiate. A few miles on there was a parking area and in it was a police car. "Pull in Ted," said Jack. "I just want to have a look." Jack got out and had a look in the car. There was nobody in it, but the door was partly open. He got back in the pickup without saying anything. "You alright Jack?" asked Ted.

"I'm OK Ted, I've got to be but sometimes it's not easy. There's no one in it, but I've a good idea who would have been."

They drove off steadily, not saying much until they got to near where they wanted to be. They were on the hill-top now and had a beautiful view over the valley right down to the river. "Right Ted," said Jack. "You see that farm over there, well their place is two fields this side of that and the lane to it should be somewhere here."

"Is that it just up there?" said Ted.

"I think so," replied Jack. "Just go on a bit, yes, that's it, turn in there."

Ted turned into the lane but didn't get far as there was a tree down right across the lane, about fifty metres in front of them. "Well, we're not going to move that," said Ted. "But in four wheel drive we can go across the field."

The field didn't have a gate, so Ted engaged his four-wheel drive and drove into the field just inside the hedge parallel to the road. They could see the shelter just beyond some trees and had gone about half-way when. Bang, bang bang. Ted hit the brakes, was someone shooting at them? "That's not the reception I expected," said Jack. "But hang on, who's this coming?" A figure appeared from the trees and headed down the hill towards the river. "Well, I don't know who that was, but he can't half move."

"At that speed he has to be mutant," said Ted. "But did you notice his right arm was hanging down?"

"I didn't," said Jack. "But he's gone now, shall we keep going?"

"That's what we're here for mate, let's go for it."

They approached the shelter slowly and as quietly as possible until they saw someone, and then stopped. "Sound your horn," said Jack. Ted tooted his horn with the old favourite: dah da da dah dah, dah dah. Two more people appeared, they were about a hundred meters away, one came out into the open and waved, Ted tooted back. "I think we can move in now," said Jack.

Ted stopped outside the shelter to the cautious appearance of six people. Jack recognised Bill and Wilf immediately and got out of the pickup. "Hey up lads," said Jack. "Police Sergeant Jack Bright at your service. I heard the shots, what was that all about?"

"Good to see you Jack," said Bill. "Come and meet the rest and we'll tell you about it." Jack and Ted greeted the rest of the group who they had all known about before, but not all personally.

"Who's missing; where's Mark and Colleen." said Jack.

"No one," said Bill. "They're inside, but Colleen has been shot, not bad, but some pellets in her arm."

They went in to greet Mark and Colleen and make sure she wasn't too badly injured.

Bill started by telling them that they had only been out about two months and had started settling down to what looked like being a nice quiet comfortable existence. They had walked about in the fields, gathered fruit, and shot rabbits and even fished in the river for fresh food. Bill and Wilf had shotguns and plenty of cartridges and as it had stopped raining, were just about to have a barbeque when the other visitor arrived.

The other visitor who Ted and Jack had seen running away was described by Paul as being more or less physically human, but was totally aggressive and didn't speak, but just growled and snarled. It had been before and tried to attack everybody but one of them had been on hand to fire a warning shot and it had gone. But this time it had arrived with a gun. Colleen and Claire were preparing the barbie when he turned up and as soon as they saw him, they made a run for the shelter, but he fired and luckily only winged Colleen. One of us always has a gun handy and Bill happened to be at the door at the time and got two shots off at him, and one shot got his gun arm and he dropped it and ran. "Yes, I noticed his arm hanging down when we saw him running away," said Ted.

"At least we've got another gun," said Wilf.

Ted had noticed the four vehicles parked in a neat line but overgrown with bushes. "Have you thought of getting them going Bill?" asked Ted.

"Well, we've had a look at them," replied Bill, "But without batteries, we're stumped." There were two pickups, a car and Paul's van. "I think we can help you out there," said Ted. "If you can get them pulled out into the open and free all the brakes off and a general tidy up, we can be back in a day or two, that should be OK, shouldn't it Jack?"

"Don't see why not," replied Jack.

They swapped stories for over an hour and were not sure if it was a joke or not when Jack told them about the Johnsons. But after experiencing what they just had, they couldn't wait to meet them. Pauline asked if they would like some lunch and together, they said: "Yes please." They talked some more then Jack suggested they started back and take Colleen with them so Dr Margaret could get her arm sorted out, because obviously the pellets had to be removed. Mark said he wanted to stay with his wife so Jack thought a while then decided Ken has a big house and a spare room, they could stay there. Ted's pickup had the big crew cab, so there was plenty of room for Mark and Colleen. "Right then, we'll get going," said Jack. "See you soon, bye."

Jack decided that it was a good opportunity to talk to Mark about his crane while they were travelling steadily back to the village. He told them about the mill, how Norman was going to repair the sails over winter. Ted told him about his workshop being more or less back in working order even without mains power. Mark wasn't only a welder with a mobile crane, but also a pretty good mechanic and did all his own repairs. So, he thought that between them they had a good chance of getting it working again. Colleen couldn't seem to get her head round the idea that some of their friends were centaurs, but Jack assured her it was true and they were really good people.

They were getting close to the village now and could see it in the distance. Mark and Colleen obviously knew the area and Mark suddenly realised why the centaurs were called Johnson. "Of course," he said. "Johnson's farm, we're nearly there."

"Well, we'll not go and see them now," said Jack. "I want to get Colleen to the doctor first." But they didn't have to as Norman was standing at the end of the lane. Ted pulled up. "Hi Norman," said Ted. "We've got some new friends for you, what are you doing here?"

"Oh, I'm just waiting for the kids, I saw a shig earlier, so I thought I'd go and meet them from school. Although they could both outrun a shig if they had to." Jack introduced them to each other but Mark and Colleen just sat there, speechless. "Everything all right while we were gone?" asked Jack.

"No problems," replied Norman. "Just the shig, but it just wandered off, I think it was a female."

Tony and Beth came trotting up the road. "Hi, you two, how was school?"

"It was really good today Dad, in between the other lessons Rebecca was teaching us to sing and dance, but me and Beth invented our own kind of dancing."

"Well," said Colleen. "If I hadn't just seen this with my own eyes I would never, ever have believed it."

"That's not all is it Jack," Norman said with a grin. "Come on kids, let's go for some tea."

"What did he mean?" said Mark as they moved on.

"Well, I think he meant the catfolk, I can't remember if we mentioned them when we were at your place." Jack answered.

"What on earth are catfolk?" asked Colleen. Jack started to tell them about finding Jan in the warehouse and taking him back to the mine when they reached the school. They stopped at the school as Margaret was probably still there, when Jan came out, followed by Tom and Sue.

Although the catfolk spoke quite well, they weren't very well educated and had decided to go to school and learn more, they hadn't much else to do anyway. So they joined in with rest of the children in lessons and enjoyed it.

"Hi Jan," said Jack. "Is Doctor Margaret still in there?"

"Yes," said Jan. "And Rebecca, they're just tidying up."

"Bye." And the three catfolk set off home, which was only round the corner.

"Hang on there a minute, Ted," said Jack. "I'll just tell her we're here and what's happened."

Jack told Margaret about their day and how Colleen got shot, but Rebecca was worried about her dad and told him so. But he assured her that he could take care of himself.

Down the road at Margaret's surgery, although a good doctor, she wasn't a surgeon, but she had been studying while in the shelter and got to work on Colleen's arm. She had caught five pellets not far apart, so the operation was a little tricky but with a local anaesthetic, was successful.

Ken and his wife Helen agreed to let the Black wells stay at their house for a couple of days as they had plenty of room. Ken and Mark had met before but didn't really know each other well, Ken had been a self-employed builder and hired his crane a couple of times. Dr Margaret had advised Colleen to stay for a couple of days as she wanted to make sure she didn't have an infection in her arm.

Colleen couldn't stop talking about the Johnsons and next morning asked if they could meet them as they had only seen them briefly on the way here. So, it was arranged with Norman that they went to see them but it had to be in the afternoon as Norman was busy in the morning, also they would be able to meet Tony and Beth when they left school.

So that afternoon Ken said he would take them to the Johnson's farm. Norman met them with a smile and asked Colleen how her arm was. She told him she thought Margaret had done a good job and it was going to be OK. Norman showed Mark around the farm and explained all about how they were planning the food growing, milling flour, and preserving other foods. Colleen was also getting on very well with Mary and was amazed at how well she was running the home, more or less the way she ran her own. Mary explained how the kitchen was generally the same as ordinary houses but had to be a lot bigger because of their obvious physical size. Then Tony and Beth came trotting in after school and said their hellos, but all Colleen could say was how well she thought the family had adapted to life and accepted it. Mary asked if they would like to stay for tea, but Ken explained that Helen was getting it ready and expecting them home. But Colleen promised Mary that it would be a definite appointment for the future.

During the next few days Mark and Colleen got to know all the others including the catfolk, Colleen spent a short time in the school and told the children about their time in their shelter and why her arm was in a sling. Mark got together with Ted and discussed various subjects. Mark wanted to have a look at his property and as it was not too far away Ted took him.

Ted stopped at Mark's gate. "I don't believe this," said Mark.

"Believe what?" asked Ted.

"It looks like it always does when we get back off holiday, nothing's changed." Mark had always been fairly methodical and put things away, tidied up and locked up. Now was it going to be as it always was? He'd brought his keys with him so, gate key, no problem, (he routinely oiled his locks), and the big steel gates swung open, then the workshop door. Inside, the red painted floor just had a coating of dust as had everything else, otherwise it was just as he had left it. "You know what, Ted?" Mark said.

"What's that?" replied Ted.

"I just can't wait to get back in here."

"Well, it's your crane we're going to need," Ted reminded him. "Let's have a quick look at it then we can make some arrangements to get it going." Mark agreed that it was going to be useful for some jobs and was looking forward to getting back home, as his house was also on his property.

Jack and Ted decided to call a meeting and consider what to do when they took Mark and Colleen back and see what could be done about the aggressive mutant. So, a meeting was held and it was agreed that Jack, Ted and Colin would go as Ken and Harry knew where it was in case of emergency. They decided to go in Ted's pickup truck as it had the big crew cab to seat five people. Norman was to be left in charge as he obviously couldn't go in the pickup. "I should go with you," said Norman. "I may be able to communicate with him."

"Well, the idea's good," said Jack. "But if he turns up with another gun, you're a big target and how do we get you there?" Jim remembered Frank Loxley had some horse boxes he used to hire out and as Ted's pickup had a tow bar fitted, no problem.

The horse box was agreed on and Ted and Jim went to Loxley's place and acquired a horse box. When they took it over to the Johnson's farm, Norman immediately christened it 'Johnson's taxi'.

Ted had loaded his pickup with things he said he would take, a generator, two drums of diesel and two freshly charged batteries. Norman had made up a box of fresh bread and milk from his goats as a welcome gift. Eric had also parcelled up some fresh 'shig' steaks. Ted and Jack had agreed that the hostile mutant was not going to be friendly, so Jack made sure that they all had a shot gun and plenty of cartridges and he had his handgun and a rifle.

The next morning after making sure that Ken was in radio contact with all the others in the village, it was time to go.

With Mark, Colleen and Colin in the back seat, the horse box was coupled up and Norman got into his 'taxi'. Ted closed the tailgate, "You OK, Norman?" he asked.

"Fine Ted." he replied. "Let's go."

Ted moved off steadily out of the farmyard and onto the road, then stopped, and shouted back to Norman. "Are you alright in there Norman?" Norman had the top window open at the front and shouted back. "Yes, this is great, go for it, but I've no money to pay for the fare." Ted laughed as he moved off up the road.

When they were nearing the lane where they turned into the hillside, Ted stopped. "I'm just thinking about how to approach this," said Ted.

"We must be psychic," answered Jack. "I was just going to ask you to stop and assess the situation, you three stay in the truck we'll have a word with Norman." They both got out and Norman was looking out of the window. "We're nearly there Norman," said Jack. "Just a bit further and down that lane, have you any ideas if this creature is around?"

"Don't know yet," replied Norman. "But let me out and I'll have a look around." Norman, as with the rest of his family, could sense danger if there was any in the vicinity. Ted opened the tail gate and let Norman out. He had his gun with him but handed it to Jack. "Hang on to this, will you Jack," said Norman. "I don't think there's anything about, but if there is I don't want to look aggressive."

"OK Norman," replied Jack. "But we'll not be far away."

Norman walked up the road to the end of the lane looking all around as he approached it. He just stood there for a while, looking, and listening, then turned and waved them to move up to him.

"All's quiet at the moment Jack, I think we can go in."

"Right Norman, but we'll have to leave your taxi here, because of that tree, we have to go across the field."

"No problem, I don't think anyone will steal it." Norman laughed.

Ted unhooked the trailer and moved steadily across the field up to the shelter with Norman walking alongside. They stopped outside; there was nobody about, then Mark said, "Hang on, don't get out yet, they should have seen us on the periscope, something's up." Norman was standing by Ted's open window. "I think it's OK now Mark," Norman assured him. "But something's been here recently." They all got out of the pickup just as Bill opened the main door of the shelter. "Hello again," he said, not noticing Norman at first, then, "What? I only half believed you when you told us about the Johnsons, but I can't argue with this."

"Hi, I'm Norman."

"And I'm Bill."

"And I'm Paul," said the two who had come out together. They shook hands warmly as Bill, still amazed at what he was seeing asked Norman how he had got here. Norman told him about his 'taxi' and it was at the end of the road.

The rest of the group came from the shelter when Bill shouted it was OK.

The group's interest obviously centred around Norman for a while, but Jack was always alert and started asking about what Norman had said about something being there recently. Norman said he sensed the presence of the creature that had been there previously, something he couldn't really explain but a mixture of smell and the surrounding atmosphere. But as he hadn't been here before he didn't know what it was. Bill then explained to him what he'd seen and what had happened. Norman thought for a while, then, stood quite still listening. "Something's coming," he said. "I think you should all go inside except Bill and Jack." Bill had his shot gun and Jack had his pistol.

"I'll get my rifle from the pickup," said Ted.

"OK Ted, but stay with Bill by the truck in case there's more than one of them and they're not friendly."

The hedge was quite high along the side of the lane so it wasn't possible to see anything that may be in the field from where they were. "There is something in the field Jack, coming up the hedge side, stay close to me and I'll try and communicate with it."

"Hello," said Norman in a completely different voice. "We don't want to harm you, come, and talk to me." There was a small gap in the hedge a little bit further on, but as Norman got nearly there the creature leapt through the gap and tripped, but rolled out of it, a bit commando style and fired a shot at Norman. Jack dropped down Under Norman's legs and got one shot at it which seemed to have stopped it. But as

Jack got up to go to it, the creature rolled over and tried to give jack the other barrel. But Jack was ready and fired one more to its head and it was dead.

"I didn't want to do that," said Jack. "But I didn't have much choice."

"I know what you mean, Jack," said Norman, "but don't worry too much about it because that thing was never going to be friendly."

"How do you know that?" said Jack, "and what happened to your voice?"

"I'm not sure Jack," replied Norman, "but I sensed pure aggression from it and my voice just came out in some kind of peaceful mode, which actually surprised me." By then Ted and Bill had come running up with guns ready.

"Are you two alright?" shouted Ted.

"Yes Ted," replied jack, "we're OK but it was close for a moment." They stood around looking at the creature for a couple of minutes before anyone spoke.

"It's nearly all human," said Bill, "but I thought it was the first time we saw it when it shot Colleen. It was quite like the catfolk but hairier and its head was more or less dog-like with fearsome teeth."

"Well, we can't leave it here," said Jack. "We'll take it somewhere quiet and peaceful and give it a decent burial."

"I know a good spot," said Bill. "Shall we take it now?"

"Lay it across my back and we'll take it now," said Norman. As they were lifting it onto Norman's back, Jack saw that Norman's arm was bleeding.

"Hey, you're injured Norman, why didn't you say something?"

"It's not much Jack, I just didn't quite dodge all the pellets from that shot, and a couple just grazed my arm," replied Norman.

"I've just noticed something else," said Bill, "this isn't the one that came before, he should have a wounded arm and he hasn't."

"That means there're more of them," said Jack, "we could have a small war on our hands."

Norman carried the creature to the spot under some trees where Bill had suggested and laid it down where they would bury it later.

Returning to the shelter the general conversation was about the 'wolfmen' as they had decided to call them. They generally agreed that there was probably just the one family, and these had been two brothers, but what the rest of the family consisted of was another matter, but this was only a guess. Jack jokingly suggested that it seemed to be getting a bit like the wild west and if he was the sheriff, they should form a posse and go hunting the bad guys. But in reality, it wasn't such a bad idea although it wouldn't be today. "The way I see it," said Jack, "is we're assuming there is only one family, minus one and minus two guns, so the odds are better than they were."

"If you lads can get these pickups going, because they both have four-wheel drive. Then have a quiet drive round in the general direction they came from to try and establish where they are. Then if you find them, don't get too close and leave. That might indicate we are not aggressive and leave it at that for a few days then we'll come back in force and try to meet them on friendly terms."

Pete agreed and said, "I can't think of a better idea because after surviving what we have, we don't want to end up fighting each other."

So, while the ladies prepared some lunch, the men decided to unload the pickup of generators, batteries and diesel. "Hang on a minute," said Ted. "Before we unload, let's pull the two pickups out of the rough on to a bit of good going while I have a bit of weight on to give me a bit more traction. With this weight I should be able to drag them out even if the brakes are stuck on."

"Good thinking Ted," said Bill. "It will be a lot easier for me to work on them." So, with the tow rope coupled up Ted dragged both pickups out into the open with most of the wheels sliding.

"Thanks a lot Ted," said Bill. "That's a lot easier to get at them, and I've been thinking about the diesel. If we fill all the tanks, you can take the drums back with you and bring some more next time which should keep us going for quite a while."

"Good idea, Bill," said Ted. "We've got plenty back at home."

So the truck was unloaded and then it was lunch time, the food had been taken in as soon as they arrived so the ladies had prepared a mini feast for the men.

There was quite a bit to talk about over lunch and for the next hour. As there were eleven of them plus Norman they had decided to eat outside with someone always on guard duty with a loaded gun. But all was quiet, and it was decided that Jack, Ted and Norman would return a week later.

So, it was time to leave and the 'Hillsiders' all agreed that the group from town were more than welcome at any time, but they were thinking of moving back to town in the not too distant future. They also said they wanted to make peace with the 'wolfman' creatures, mainly because they had also survived and deserved a future, whatever it may be.

All the goodbyes were made, and Ted headed up the field alongside the hedge to the gap where Norman's 'taxi' was waiting at the end of the lane.

"Colin, do you want to ride up front with Ted?" said Jack. "I just want to be a bit quiet in the back for a while."

"No problem, Jack, I can see a bit more of the road from there, I missed a bit of it coming." Colin replied. So, the horse box was coupled up, Norman got in, Ted closed the tailgate and they set off home.

Although Jack was a big, hard, police sergeant he also had a big heart. He had to try and get his head around the fact that he had recently killed someone, or something, because it was at least half human.

The journey home was fairly quiet, with only some conversation between Ted and Colin. But on arriving back at the village after dropping Norman and his 'taxi' at the farm, Jack had already assumed his role of authority.

"Can you drop me off first Ted?" he said, "I'll leave the rest to you for today; I'm just having a bit of tea and an early night."

"No problem, Jack. Listen mate, it was you or him and I'm just more than pleased you're still here. Have a drop of that brandy you found, see you in the morning, bye."

The next day started with Jack's usual radio calls to everyone, and all replied back with no problems. Jack appeared to be back to his usual self but yesterday was something that would be with him for quite a while.

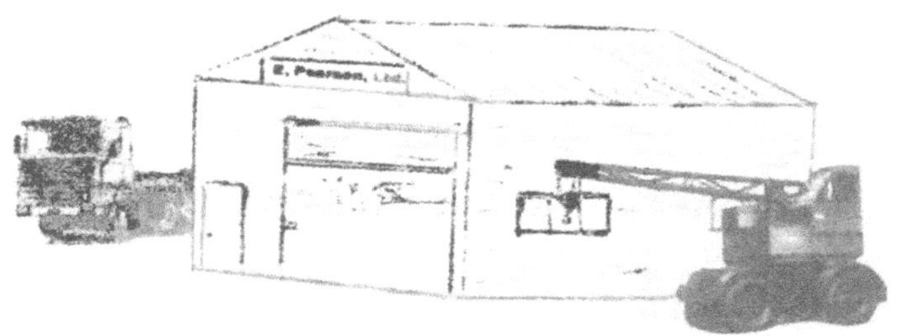

Ted's Place

Ted had always been a keen vintage vehicle collector, hence his truck and crane, but being Ted, between him and Jim they were kept in good working order and reliable. Norman was more than impressed with Ted's place and was just a little bit envious he couldn't be a bit more involved in the machinery. But he accepted he was what he was and helped in all the other work. However. Jack and Ted had decided to have a ride into town for a look round some of the other places.

"Jack to Norman, you there, mate?"

"Morning, Jack how are you today?" replied Norman. "I know yesterday must have been a bit traumatic for you."

"I'm OK I just have to get used to it and although it may happen again, I hope it doesn't, but we have to be prepared for anything. Anyway, I just wondered if you needed Jim today as we want him to have a look at the digger, it's playing up a bit and me and Ted are going into town for a look round."

"No, I'm just doing a bit of planning for the next couple of months, crops, fields, etc. then maybe get a bit done on the windmill sails." replied Norman.

"OK mate so can you keep your ears on while we're away in case we get out of range."

"No problem," said Norman, "but just be careful, you never know what may be round the comer."

"OK," said Jack, "I'll call you later."

So, Jack with his handgun and Ted with a shot gun, they set off to town.

Jack had known some people who had built a shelter on the west side of town which was on a hillside looking west. He told Ted about them and decided to go there first as there were either two or three families who had planned to use it. When they got there, all was quiet and abandoned as it had been left, but the shelter entrance was clearly visible, so they went over. On the front was the expected solar panel and an air vent but no sign of a speaker system. But Ted had a closer look and said there looked to be one in the vent. "Let's give it a try," said Jack. It was just inside the vent grill, so jack found a twig and poked it in to give it a tap. Jack tapped the speaker and said, "Hello in there, is there anyone there?" There was no reply, so they waited a few minutes and tried again. "Hello in there, is anyone there?" This time there was a crackling noise and some muffled sounds but not making any sense. Jack tapped the speaker again and just got a similar noise. So, Jack just spoke very clearly into the thing and said, "This is police sergeant, Jack Bright, we have been out a while and if you are OK you can start opening up, but we have to be going now so we'll call again tomorrow and hopefully see you then."

On the way back they decided to call at a supermarket to see if there were any signs of anyone been to it, and maybe pick up a few things. When they got there the car park had a few cars in it and one even had a body inside. The main shop's front door wasn't even locked, but it didn't look as though anyone had been before them. So, they had a look inside and filled a trolley with some things that they didn't have in the village shop, mostly cleaning stuff and some tinned food. They also had a look round the clothing part and both agreed that the women would like to come and pick up a few things.

Ted dropped Jack off at home just as Steven was coming home, he'd spent the morning with Jim sorting the digger out and with a few tips from Jim had been busy with job of burying bodies at their own homes where possible. He'd had one of the other men with him to do that and as there were no coffins, the bodies were wrapped in whatever bedding they had.

Liz met Ted at the door, and he showed her what he had got from the supermarket which they had decided they would go to shop in the morning.

Jack called Norman to tell him what they had found and asked him if he could do the same tomorrow as they were going to town again to meet whatever survivors there were. He would also bring them up to date with everything and hopefully arrange a meeting of everyone in the near future. Jack's wife, Wendy, said would it be possible to go with them to look round the supermarket. Jack thought a minute and said, "Why not, as we're not going to stay long over there why don't you call Liz and see if she would like to come as well." So Wendy called Liz and agreed to meet in the morning.

The next morning Jack asked his daughter, Rebecca, about safety at the school as now the other men were all doing other jobs. Well Liz had been a bit worried about Pete and Jane being at school and had got together with Margaret and Rebecca and given them some tuition on shotguns as she had been a member of the local clay shooting club. Jack didn't know about this, so Rebecca said, "Don't worry Dad, we may not be commandos, but thanks to Liz, we know what to do, we have two shotguns at the school."

So Ted dropped Pete and Jane off at school and, with Liz, arrived at Jack's place. Wendy met them at the door and said, "Jack will be out in a minute, he's just checking with Norman."

"Jack to Norman, you up yet?" Jack said laughingly.

"Morning Jack, I've been up all day, where have you been?" Norman replied with a similar joking tone.

"Just checking as we're ready to go to town, what are you doing today?" said Jack.

"Jim's coming over today we're going to see if we can get some winter seed sown as it's a good day," replied Norman. "But we'll still keep out ears on the village, take care."

So, the four set off to town and went first to the shelter they visited yesterday. On arrival they were surprised to see two men already out, looking round who greeted them enthusiastically.

"Good morning, Jack," said the first man, "I'm Arthur Burton, you may not remember, but we have met once before, but I'll not go into why," he said with grin.

"And I'm Keith Cross," said the other one. "Our wives are still trying to get ready to take it the fact we are still alive and kicking on the outside again." So, the two wives came out and introductions all round went well. Jack went on to tell them about the Johnsons, which was taking quite a bit of accepting, but Liz and Wendy together convinced them they were fantastic people, even though they were half horse.

The eight of them spent about an hour swapping stories with Jack, not particularly laying down the law, but bringing them fully up to date with all that had been done and what was best for the future. Ted told them he could possibly find a vehicle for them in the near future and let them know when. "We'll get a selection of fresh food for you in a couple of days and bring it up for you," said Jack, "and check with Norman for anything else he may have growing."

So, it had been a good meeting and the four moved on to the supermarket. Wendy and Liz headed straight for the clothing department, and they could be heard all over expressing their excitement. Most of the clothing was in its original packing and still in perfect condition. So, they loaded up two trolleys and met up with the men at Ted's pickup. It had been a good morning and they would be home for lunch.

Meanwhile Jim had been with Norman and together they had managed to get the seed drill back into working order and made a good start on getting the com seed in for next year's crop.

Well Norman had been studying early farming from the old Mr. Johnson's books and decided that everything had to go back to the early days of farming. So, he had redrawn the whole farm in his office which he had created in the part of the shelter. He had drawn a full-scale map of the entire area and planned to plant more hedges to tum the extra-large fields into smaller ones. This would be much easier to manage and there weren't too many people to feed anyway, but for now he had marked out three plots of about ten acres each for com, potatoes, and vegetables. But the rest of the fields would be left as they are for now: Norman had wanted to have all the other fields ploughed and left to the weather over winter, but Jim had reminded him that although they had plenty of diesel at the moment, he didn't want to use it up unnecessarily, so decided to just plough one extra field for this year.

Back at Jack's house Wendy got what clothing she wanted from what they had taken and left the rest in Ted's pickup for Liz to sort out later. "How about some lunch?" said Wendy, "I can soon knock up a salad."

"Thanks Wendy," replied Ted, "but I want to get home and just have something quick and go down to Norman's to see how him and Jim have got on and tell Norman about the other survivors and see if he can get some fruit and vegetables together for these other people and I'll get Eric to make up a pack of meat"

"Right Ted," said Jack, "so I think I'll go see them the day after tomorrow and I must remember to tell them about church on Sunday."

Ted arrived at Norman's farm just as him and Jim were going to finish off the com planting.

"Hi, you two," said Ted, "how's it going?"

"We've nearly got it all done," replied Norman, "just a bit to finish off as I had to go back to the barn for one more sack of seed."

"That's great," said Ted, "now, Jim, how's Steven getting on with the burials, is the digger OK now?"

"As far as I know," said Jim, "he's got Collin and Ken with him today and I haven't heard from him, so I guess he's OK." Ted told them about the other people they had found and asked Norman if he could make up a pack of fruit and veg. for them and Jack would pick it up tomorrow ready for going back to them the day after.

"They didn't believe us when Jack told them about you," said Ted to Norman. "But they will on Sunday, if they agree to come to church, we forgot to tell them about that, but Jack will when he goes."

"I remember Arthur Burton," said Jim, "it'll be good to see him again."

So, village life was getting more organised and better every day and time for Jack to take the supplies to their new found survivors. Eric had made up a good pack of meat and with Norman's vegetables Jack went on his own for this trip. They were all sat outside having a morning coffee when Jack got there. "Morning all," said Jack, "you must have been to the supermarket."

"Seemed like a good idea after you told us," replied Keith, "and we were a bit wary, so Arthur took his shotgun." So, the goods were received with open arms and they all agreed to attend church on Sunday as long as someone could pick them up.

Sunday morning came and Harry had volunteered to go and pick them up as he knew where they were. "Good morning to you all," said Harry when he arrived, "it's great to see more people reappearing, and especially when it's someone I know, how are you, Keith?"

"Really good to see you, Harry," replied Keith. Keith had used Harry's bank before the trouble began.

"Your next surprise is coming up," said Harry.

"What's that?" asked Arthur.

"Meeting the Johnsons." replied Harry. When they arrived at the church, the four of them just stood in disbelief at seeing a family of four centaurs stood in the church grounds talking to other people.

After the service the women had decided to welcome the new friends with some refreshments and set up some tables outside.

"We didn't think the Good Lord would mind if we got together here for a reunion," said Margaret, "so with a little wine and some of Ken's cider to wash it down, let's have a snack."

So after an enjoyable couple of hours, it was time to go. "I'll take them back home jack," said Harry, "as long as you aren't going to arrest me for drink driving." Jack just laughed.

Jack had warned Keith, Arthur, and their wives about the shigs being around and also told them about the 'cat folk', so they would not be worried if they happened to meet them. So, he made sure they had a shot gun each and ample cartridges. He also suggested they considered moving to a home of their choice a bit nearer to the rest of them. Then they would be nearer the fresh food supply and would be available to help out with anything that needed doing. They agreed and would start looking round when Ted got them fixed up with a car.

But now it's late Autumn and the farm is more or less settled down for winter, so Norman is spending most of his time being a joiner. The windmill sails were an ongoing job, but he also did repair jobs for anyone who needed something doing.

Then it was a matter of the hillsiders; they were keen to get back home, but at the same they still had the wolf people to consider. Bill had managed to get two of the pickup trucks running and him and Mark had been for a brief look round where the wolf people stayed but hadn't seen anything moving so they came back still wondering about them.

So, Jack got together with Ted and Norman to decide when they would return to the hill side group. It was to be the next day as they had not much else to do for a while.

Next morning Ted picked Jack up, then Colin and went round to Norman's farm to collect him. "Morning all," said Norman, "are we all agreed on how we approach this as it could be a bit tricky."

"More or less," replied jack, "but I think we will have to play it by ear for a start."

So Norman's 'taxi' was coupled up and with him in, they set off to the hill side.

On arrival Ted gave the usual toct on the horn and Mark came out to greet them. "Good morning," he said, "how are you all?"

"We're all well," replied Jack. "Are you all OK?"

"Yes, we're all fine but we weren't sure when you were coming." Then the rest came out to greet them and it was time to decide on the tactics for contacting the wolf people. As Bill had managed to get two of the pickups running, they decided to go to them in force. So, it would be three pickups and

Norman. So, with Jack in Ted's, Bill and Pete in another and Mark and Collin in the other one Norman would trot alongside. Wilf was to stay behind with the women to keep an eye out for any trouble.

Mark led the 'posse', (A bit like the wild west) nice and steady for Norman to keep up, as he knew more or less where they were. They got to where they wanted to be, and all cautiously got out. "What's the situation, Norman," asked Jack.

"All's quiet at the moment, Jack," replied Norman.

So, six men with guns standing in front of three pickups and Norman the centaur, also with a gun, standing in front was quite as impressive sight and not something to be argued with.

"Tell you what," said Norman, "blow the truck's horns, all three." So, Ted, Bill and Mark reached through the open windows and pressed the horn, then back in line with others. They waited a couple of minutes, then a figure appeared from behind some bushes, then two more, one was holding a gun and one had an arm wrapped up. They couldn't make out if they were male or female as they looked the same. Norman stepped to one side and the other six pointed their guns at them.

The creature with the gun lowered it but didn't put it down, Norman held his gun in the air then handed it to Jack. "We want to talk to you," said Norman, "we don't want to harm you, can you speak?" Norman started to walk towards them making sure he wasn't between them and his gang. The one with the gun started to growl and then broke into a very low harsh, but loud voice and said, "Where is my man, what have you done with my man?"

"I'm sorry, but I have to tell you he's dead," replied Norman, "he tried to kill us and one of my men had to shoot back."

"Which one did it?" the creature asked and pointed his gun at the six.

"It's not important who did it, but you with the bad arm already shot one of our women, and if you don't put your gun down you will all be shot." The creature looked at the other two and laid her gun on the ground. "Thank you," said Norman, "just walk away from the gun and we will talk."

The other six joined Norman and heard the creature's story. They had been reared in a shelter by a family of five and some animals. The others had all died but they had somehow survived and been out of the shelter quite a while but had got used to it. So, after a good talk and agreeing to be friendly to anyone else they may see, Jack said they could keep their gun for hunting as they didn't want to leave the place they were happy at.

CONFRONTING THE CANINES

So, the six of them said their cautious goodbyes and went back to the shelter to tell their findings to Wilf and the women. The women were obviously pleased to hear that they were not going to be attacked by them again and the group sat down for a well-deserved lunch.

The next subject was about moving back to the village; Mark was more than keen to be going, as was Bill. Wilf and Paul weren't in such a big hurry, but didn't fancy staying in the shelter without Mark and Bill. "Tell you what," said Jack, "you've plenty of diesel now so how about coming over one day and you can have a look at your old places and maybe look round for somewhere else."

"I can't wait," said Mark, "today's Tuesday, so what about Thursday?" They all agreed, and it was time for Jack's crew to go home. So, with Norman in his 'taxi', they set off back to the village.

The rest of the village were pleased to hear they were to going to have more people around as some of them knew each other.

Next day Ted decided to have a look round for a car as he had promised the two couples in town. He decided on a quite nice diesel car and him and Jim went to sort it out with a battery and fuel. Now before the trouble the government had been trying to get rid of diesel and petrol cars and have everybody driving electric cars. But this was proven to be completely impractical as thousands of people had no means of charging them. As nearly all trucks were running on diesel, many people had stuck with diesel or petrol. There were some beautiful petrol-engine cars parked all over, but petrol goes off with age and there just wasn't any. So they got the car ready and took it to town where they were to be greeted by some very happy people. Arthur had been a keen mechanic and owned a car recycling business, while Keith had been in the car trade with a nice little dealership.

"Thanks a million," said Arthur, "we'll manage with this one for now until we've got to know how and where to go from here, then Keith and me can look round for another one."

The next morning Liz had agreed to join Caroline at school as Margaret was going to the old mine to check on the old folk. As they were out of radio range, she was going to try and convince them to move to the village as they would be much safer and have more friends to see if they needed anything. Harry took Margaret over and the two old couples agreed to move to the small holding with the 'cat folk' Jan, Tom, and Sue. They couldn't all get in the car, so Harry said he would arrange for them to be picked up the next day.

During this time there had been a quite scary time at the school. At the mid-morning break, a young shig had found its way to the playground and was starting to attack one of them. The kids quickly ran inside but Jan, Tony and Beth stayed there and tried to chase it away. But it started to charge at Beth so Jan tried to distract it as he could easily outrun it, so Tony turned quickly and with a lightening back kick knocked it against the school wall. As it was getting up to make another charge, Beth turned and gave it another kick towards Tony who was ready and once again kicked it to the wall. Then Liz was there with her gun and screamed, "Move, you two." And fired one shot at it, then the other barrel for good measure. The shig was dead, but fortunately it was only a young one.

"You two are lucky it wasn't an adult," said Liz, "you could have been killed."

"Well, we've seen Dad tackle one and knew that although they are very powerful, they are not very quick, so I thought as it was a young one, we could handle it."

"It's OK Rebecca," shouted Liz, "we've got it." So Rebecca and the kids all came out to have a look and gave Jan, Tony and Beth a big hug.

Jan, being older didn't attend school on a regular basis as he was mostly busy working on their smallholding, but he wanted to learn more so went when he could.

The next morning, Jack had arranged to meet the hillsiders at Norman's farm as it was the first place on the way coming in. When they arrived, Norman showed them all that was happening and what was planned for the future. Then, on to Mark's place as it was next, he and Coleen wanted to stay for a while and have a good look round and make a list of what wanted doing. The rest then went to the village to see their own places and make decisions on what was to be next. Paul and Pauline had lived in a village just north of town, so they were having a good look round to find a place in the village. Bill and Wilf with their wives decided to go back to their old places as they weren't too bad and a lot of the stuff inside was still in good condition. However, they would all have to commute between the hillside and the village until they got them habitable. They agreed it would only take a few days and the villagers were ready to help if needed.

So, with goodbyes said in the village they picked Mark and Coleen up, then on to Norman's place where Mary had a meal waiting for them before they went back to their shelter.

When the two pickups turned into the lane going to the shelter, Bill noticed one of the canines with a gun in the field, it just stood there until the trucks got to the shelter. All eight got out and Bill and Mark walked cautiously to the edge of the field as the others went to the shelter. Bill had his gun but just held it low, but the canine just stood and looked at them for a couple of seconds then seemed to bow to them, turned and walked away. It appeared they really did want to be friendly.

The next three days saw the eight of them coming in the morning and back to their shelter in the afternoons. Then on the Saturday two pickup trucks left the hillside shelter and headed for the village. They called in briefly at Norman's farm just to say hello and let him know they bad arrived. Bill dropped Mark and Colleen of at their place then into the village to be happily greeted by whoever saw them.

So, the village community was growing and the extra skills that had come with them were readily accepted. Wilf, as a builder, immediately got on well with Norman and helped him with jobs that may involve a bit of climbing. Bill spent a lot of time with Ted and Mark was busy sorting bis crane out with the help of Ted and Bill. Now Paul and Pauline had been up to their old place in one of the pickups to load up with a lot of things from Paul's workshop. Apart from being a good electrician and solar power engineer, he was also a keen radio ham and had been in touch with people all over the world. So, he had chosen a house with a large garage that he could use as his new workshop.

His first job was to erect a large ariel as he was sure there would be someone else out there with the same idea. Well, television was completely out of the question, but some of them still had radios that they had listened to. Jim's wife, Jean, had said she used to listen to a radio station in Sheffield. So, Paul asked if he could borrow the radio for a while, just to try a few ideas. He had his own receivers and transmitters anyway, but sometimes one works better than another.

The next day was Sunday, and the church had a much larger congregation. Although some of them hadn't been particularly religious before, they all went and thanked God for their survival.

Now as the community was growing there was a need for more electricity and there were no more small generators to be found. But Paul came to the potential rescue and told them about an occasion in his village when the main power line had to be repaired. The electricity supply company had brought in a massive generator and connected it to the pole where the main supply came into the village. The generator was on wheels and was usually towed behind a big truck. So Paul got together with Jack and decided to go to the depot and have a look and see what they could find.

Sure enough, at the depot, there were two big generators on wheels parked side by side, so Paul opened the side panel of one and said it looked to be in fairly good condition, but it would need a good going over by Ted. "One small problem," said Jack, "how do we get it home?"

"Looks like a job for Ted," replied Paul, "but hang on a minute, Ted's bloke Jim is with Norman's tractor."

"Great," said Jack, "let's go tell them."

Jack told Ted and Bill what they had found and asked if they were available to go tomorrow and get one on the generators road worthy as they both had a flat tyre. Paul would go with them and choose the better on the two and Ted said he would talc batteries and fuel to try them first.

Next day, "Jack to Norman, you there, mate?" It was Jack's first call of the day.

"Sure Jack, what's up?"

"No problems, but hopefully tomorrow we need the tractor if Jim's not using it." Jack told Norman what they were doing and then realised there would be Ted's big generator spare, so it could go to the farm as the village supply didn't go to the farm. Ted, Bill, and Paul returned with the good news that they had got one of the generators going and Jim was to pick it up in the morning. Jim arrived at the electricity depot next day and Ted was there waiting to give him a hand and follow him back to the pole where the main supply came into the village. There, Paul was already checking the wiring ready to connect the generator. But before that could be done Paul had told them this would not be for a while as the whole village had to be gone over and all properties that weren't occupied had to be disconnected as lots of things could have been left switched on or wiring had been damaged. So, Paul asked Ted and Bill if they would help and showed them what to do so it wouldn't be a big job to reconnect if someone wanted to move in again.

A few days later they had all been done and it was time to couple up and switch on. Now Ted was on main line the big generator could go to Norman's farm, but it was on Ted's old scrap trailer which had all the tyres flat and in a pretty bad state. But Jim being Jim said he would get it movable and did just that. He tried inflating the tyres and had no success except for the last two, "Typical," he said, "it's always the last one, in this case two, but they'll do." So Ted gave him a hand to remove all the others and left the trailer standing on just two wheels.

"I'm not bothered about brakes," said Ted, "the generator's not too heavy for the two wheels, so we'll have a nice steady ride to the farm and the trailer can stay there."

Ted delivers the generator for Norman on his scrap trailer

Now, as winter was approaching, there was the matter of keeping warm. Most of the children and the Johnsons had never experienced frost and snow. So, a meeting was held to discuss what they could do. Mark, being a welder by trade had not only done electric, but lots of gas welding and suggested they went to the dealer who had supplied his oxygen and various gasses. It was agreed that Harry and Ken would look round town to find electric and gas heaters, while Mark and Ted would go and see if there were still any bottles of gas. They were not disappointed, although there were lots of empties, there were still plenty of full ones of propane and butane. So, they loaded up their pickup with bottles of propane for now to work any heaters Harry and Ken had acquired. They also took a couple of bottles of propane for anyone who had a gas cooker in their old house, then they had a choice. Harry and Ken came back with the pickup loaded with a choice of electric and gas heaters.

So now the villagers had a choice of gas or electric for heating and cooking.

However, everyone was warned to use the gas sparingly as it wouldn't last forever, and another supply had to be found. There was also the diesel to be considered, although they had plenty at the moment, they would have to get more, but that would be a job in the Spring. The big village generator did use quite a lot of diesel; but Bill and Paul had made up a battery powered timer switch so it started up at six o clock in the morning and switched off at ten in the evening.

However, Jack and Ted had another ride out to the oil refinery and found some more of the trucks were full. There was only one artic trailer full, the others were 4, 6 and 8 wheelers and some of those were paraffin or petrol. So the next job was to see if they could refill their trailers from the large round storage tanks but the normal filling place was out of the question as it was all powered by electricity. But Ted said he knew where he could get a diesel-powered pump and rig up something to connect to the big tank. This could be done later so the first job was to get the other artic tanker home, it didn't look too bad so Ted said him and Jim would come back the next day and hopefully bring it home.

Jack was still the authority and kept a good check on all firearms and ammunition, but asked the help of Harry to be a more or less secretary and keep a file on all outgoing stuff. Food, fuel, ammo' etc., not really checking on the people, but just getting an idea of daily and weekly needs.

Then, with winter approaching there wasn't much to do outside, but most days two of the men would have a ride out to various places to see if they could find anything of interest or indeed, any more survivors.

Then came the first frost which the children didn't like, but when it snowed, they loved that; the Johnsons had only read about it but just accepted it.

Then it was time for Christmas, and it was decided to have a party in the school, but the bonus was it did snow so they actually had a white Christmas. The whole community went to church on Christmas morning and then to the party for the rest of the day and into the evening. There was plenty of food and drink as Ken had made a nice batch of beer and cider, also Keith had brought a good selection of whisky, rum, and classic wines from the supermarket.

So, the year came to a very satisfactory end with another party on New Year's Eve.

Spring arrived and the village was getting back to normal. During the winter, Paul had been busy on his radio and had actually been talking to someone in Texas who he had been in touch with before.

Norman had done some more work on the windmill sails when it hadn't been too cold in his workshop. The school had continued running as normal. The old folk from the mine had settled in with Jan, Tom, and Sue at the small holding. Keith and Arthur had decided to stay in their old homes in town which weren't far from their shelter. Ted had fixed them up with a spare generator as they weren't on the mains, but they also had gas as well. Jack had also acquired another police radio for them so they could stay in touch and Ted had fixed them up with a car, so they were OK.

Mark had got his place, which was between the village and Norman's farm, more or less back to how it was, and he and Coleen were happy there. The village shop had had its own bakery at the back so Liz wanted to get it going again. She had helped out in the shop and also at the bakery anyway and as she enjoyed cooking again on good cookers, she said she would take two or three times a week and run the shop more or less as it had been run before. Eric's butchers' shop was only next door but one so a little bit of normality was returning.

Now, money was of no use whatsoever, but Harry had thought of an idea to keep monotony down as much as possible. He had been to his bank and come home with a large amount of money and distributed it all round with an explanation. Everyone got £1000, just for fun but it would be used as normal, basically to break the boredom. Liz and Eric quoted really low prices for their goods and the money was returned to Harry. Then Harry would pay anyone 'wages' for whatever they had done for the village. Keith got to know about it and came down to Eric's shop one day for some meat and said the last lot was great and paid him £100. "Where have you got that from?" asked Eric.

Keith just laughed and said, "I raided the tills at the supermarket." This went on for a while but gradually faded out except for the kids, who were taught values and respect for others by Margaret and Rebecca.

The diesel situation had been dealt with, Ted and Jim had been to the refinery and got the other artic tanker home and been back and even got two of the eight wheelers running and home. Next door to Ted's place had been a civil engineering company with a big yard so Ted used it to park the tankers. They had also been to another gas dealer's and brought home as many bottles as they had.

Remember, this is a story of survival and a matter of first come, first served.

Eric's wife Betty had helped him in the butcher's, but also had a small part of it selling fresh fish and asked him if he thought they could get any. Eric knew George had been a keen angler so went to see him one day and asked if he had any ideas. Well George said he had already thought about it and fancied a ride over to the pond he used to go to but didn't want to go on his own. Eric wasn't very interested in fishing but said Colin might be. So, the two got together and decided on a day fishing at the pond. They did manage to catch a couple of small ones but not much else until just before they were ready to pack up when George caught a nice big carp. Although carp are not the best fish for the table, they are still a quite nice white fish and acceptable when there is nothing else. So that evening it was fish and chips for George and Eric's families.

When Jim heard of this, he had a think as he was also a big fan of fish and chips. He didn't say anything to anyone except Bill who also kept it quiet that they would come up with something to make the day for most. They told the rest they were just going for a look round, but they went to the bus depot. They were to choose the best minibus they could, try to get it going and if possible, bring it home. They had taken all the things they needed, tools, batteries, fuel, jacks to change wheels etc. They did it, so Jim set off home in his minibus with Bill following in the pickup.

They were greeted with, "What's that for?" by Jim's wife, Jean.

"So we can all go for a day out somewhere different," replied Jim.

"I'm sure most of us like fish and chips so whoever would like to go, we can have a ride out to the river and see if we can catch some real fish."

Bill had told him that at the brief chat with the canines, they loved fish and caught lots near where they lived. So that was to be the next venture for whoever wanted to go.

Meanwhile Jack had been considering safety and been round to both gun dealers and brought all the firearms and ammunition they had back to his place. Then he got Ted to store them all in a large steel container in the yard next to his where the tankers were. This was then securely locked and only Ted and Jack had keys. However, he wanted to go further and collect all other firearms from the area. So, with the help of the firearms register he recruited Harry, Ted and Mark to spend a few days going round all properties that had held a firearms licence and collect everything, all arms and ammunition. For safety reasons they would work in pairs, him with harry and Ted with Mark. This was done and everything was stored in the steel container.

Next Job

The next job was going to need a few hands, it was time to fit the other two sails to the windmill. Norman, with some help from Wilf, had done an excellent job of making two new ones.

Fixing day came and as they had been made in Norman's large barn, the tricky bit was getting them out onto Ted's trailer. But Norman had thought of that and made them one on each side of the barn so a trailer could back into it between the two. He had made them with the heavy end near the door, so there was just room for Steven to get the long-armed digger in to lift that bit on. Ted had to uncouple the trailer and move out for Steven to do this, then four men could lift the other end and swing it round onto the trailer. They hoped to get one done one day and the other one the next.

Next morning Ted arrived at Norman's farm in his truck to collect the first sail and George, Bill, Wilf, and Jim had also arrived in Jim's pickup with all the necessary tools for the job. Mark said he would be at the mill with his crane when they got there.

Mark's Crane

Ted delivers the first sail

So now the mill was back to full power when it was windy. They were all really pleased with how the job had gone and the great job Norman and Wilf had done making the sails. George was delighted that he could now be, albeit only part time, a proud miller.

Back to its original beauty

Meanwhile Paul had been busy on has radio and been talking to the chap in Texas again. He had also been listening to jean's radio and actually heard some music, so he fine-tuned it in and heard a voice broadcasting. It really was someone using the old Sheffield radio frequency, but the signal wasn't good, possibly because of lack of power. He tried to find a way to reply to the signal but didn't have any success but kept going back to it now and then. However, it was a fact that there were survivors in Sheffield.

George fancied a day river fishing and got together with Jim and decided to organise a trip to the river with anyone else who wanted to go. He'd been to the sports shop and acquired a few more rods and things, so the day was arranged for Saturday.

Saturday arrived and the bus was nearly full as some just wanted to go for the ride as George had said the best place would be where the Canines lived as there was a good bend in the river and ideal for fishing. Norman was a little envious that he couldn't go this time but Jim sad he would sort it out for next time by fitting a tow bar to the bus then his family could all go in his 'taxi'.

Forever cautious Jack suggested for safety reasons that Ted and Liz took their guns with them as he was still a little unsure about the Canines. He was never without his pistol anyway, always wary, and ready for the unexpected.

The bus arrived at the hillsider's shelter so they had just one field to cross to the river passing where the Canine's lived. The Canines heard them coming but couldn't see what it was as they were just over the brow of the hill and not visible from the hillsider's shelter. So, the village crowd set off across the field to be greeted by the canines who were all out to see who or what it was. One had a gun but put it down on the ground as soon as it saw Jack. The villagers who hadn't met them were not sure what to make of them, but just smiled and said hello as they walked by.

The day had been good with quite a few fish being caught, so it looked like being fish and chips all round tonight.

Paul hadn't been with them on the fishing trip but had been busy on his radios. He had spent most of the time trying to contact the Sheffield signal without success and decided to just listen to the music. However, while he was busy doing something else, the music stopped and the voice came on again, a bit clearer this time. To his amazement the voice said, "Hello out there, if anyone is listening, I now have a better ariel and anyone with the equipment can call me." And gave a frequency that was easy for Paul to find. So, he had been talking to someone in Sheffield and discovered that there were quite a few survivors who had been in a large shelter and were getting on with life steadily.

Norman had remembered about the old Mr. Johnson telling him about another farmer who had kept goats. It was about two miles across the fields so him and Tony decided to go and have a look and see if anything had survived.

Norman had showed Tony how to use guns, so they set off for a morning exploring, Norman with a rifle and Tony with a shot gun. When they got close to the farm all seemed quiet and peaceful, but Norman sensed something was about, so he just said, "Hang on a minute Tony, let's just wait and see if anything's moving."

"OK, Dad," replied Tony, "but I think there's something behind the house." They stood quietly for a while then a cow came wondering out from behind the house. It looked quite normal, so they walked slowly over to it and it didn't seem bothered at all, so Tony went right up to it and stroked it gently while Norman looked it over. Then Norman remembered old Mr Johnson telling him about a farmer friend in the next village who had joined up with some others and built a big shelter a few miles away. They had decided to keep cattle and sheep as well as chickens, so he wondered if this was one of theirs. But why would it be here, it must have just strayed from the farm where it was born. Then a calf came round from behind the house and went to the cow which seemed to be its mother.

"You know what this means Tony," said Norman, "the calf must have a father somewhere." Then across a field he saw a bull plodding steadily towards them.

"I guess you're thinking what I am, Dad," Tony said, "we could do with them at home, but how do we get them there?"

"The other thing is if the other farmer's crowd survived, why have they let these animals wander off?"

"They must have opened the shelter to let them out, but what about them?" This was something he was going to have to discuss with Jack.

"Anyway, I think we'll have to walk them home, but we haven't time today," said Norman, "but I'll tell the others about them, and we'll come back tomorrow."

Next morning Norman and Tony set off to the place they had seen the cattle and they were in luck; the cattle had walked a bit nearer to where the two were coming from. "I think I'm going to enjoy this," said Tony, "it'll be a bit like the Wild West American cowboys round up I read about in that book." So the two of them gently persuaded the bull, cow and calf the walk back to Norman's place and into the paddock which was the only field with a complete fence all round.

Jim had been thinking about the fishing trip and fitting a tow bar to the bus so Norman could go next time. That would be fine but what if all four wanted to go, the horse box would only hold two. So, he had a word with Ted for any suggestions and Ted said he knew of a quite rich farmer whose family had all been involved in horses and had a very large, motorised horse box. It was about five miles away but if it was still there it would hold four horses and had a living compartment at the front. Ted also said he heard that well before the trouble started, the whole family had moved to a Pacific Island somewhere where there was little chance of a bomb dropping. They had planned to build a super-size shelter with the help of the locals and invite them to stay with them.

Anyway, they decided to go and have a look and to their delight saw the horse box standing there just waiting to be taken away. "What if they survived and want to come back?" said Jim.

"I don't think British Airways will be back in business just yet," replied Ted, with a grin. They had taken batteries and fuel with them, and Jim had no trouble starting it. It had one flat tyre, but it carried its own spare which was OK, so after changing that they were ready to go. This had been an unbelievable bit of good luck and took it back to Ted's yard.

"We'll not tell Norman about it yet," said Ted, "and tell the others to keep it quiet for now."

"Good idea Ted, because I've been thinking about something else which I'll also keep to myself for now, I'm going to call it 'The Johnson Bus'," replied Jim.

Jim's Johnson Bus

So, village life was getting back to more or less normal, although in a rather primitive way. Norman's cattle had settled in their new field, and he had asked if anyone in the village had ever milked a cow. Dairies had all been mechanised and cows had been milked mechanically and his family were not built for low down jobs, it would need someone who could sit down. Eric said he hadn't done it himself but had seen it done and his wife Betty said she wouldn't mind doing it if she had a hand. Wilt's wife Clair she would work with Betty on a day each rota, so Eric took them both to Norman's farm to 'introduce' them to the cow and get an idea of the situation. Then he took them to a hardware shop, and they got new buckets, a couple of funnels and from various places, got stocked up with bottles. Soon there would hopefully be fresh milk which no one had had for quite a while.

That was agreed and as the paddock was next to the farmyard there was a small shed which opened into the yard and the paddock, this would be used as a dairy. So, Betty and Clair took it in turns to do the milking and brought it back in bottles to Eric's fridge.

They had been having boiled wheat, but now they could have it done in milk which is an old country breakfast meal called frumenty. Also, Norman had found some oats but kept it for seed so they could have more when it was ready. This would be rolled in an old portable vintage rolling mill which was driven by a vintage tractor's pulley wheel, then hopefully, porridge for breakfast.

Jim had got the minibus fitted with a tow bar and another day fishing was arranged so this time Norman and Tony went with them in Norman's 'taxi'. This time they were actually joined by the 'canines' although they didn't get too closely involved, but the day turned out to be a good one.

Then as spring was getting warmer Jim decided to tell Ted what his other idea was. "What do you think about a day at the seaside Ted?" said Jim. "Some of the kids and the Johnsons have never seen the sea."

"Now that's a great idea," replied Ted, "we might even see someone else."

It was Saturday, so Ted said we could tell them all after church next day. After church on Sunday the idea was greeted with lots of enthusiasm and agreed to go next Saturday if the weather was good. Obviously, the Johnsons were a little bit disappointed as it looked like they were not going to be able to go. "Don't worry Norman," said Ted, "we'll work something out before next Saturday." Only Ted and Jim knew about the 'Johnson Bus' as Jim had parked it behind the tankers in the yard next to Ted's and no one had been to Ted's yard anyway.

It was Friday afternoon. "Afternoon Norman," said Ted. "About the seaside tomorrow, we've thought of something that might work, so when Betty's finished milking if you four can come down to the village we'll check it out." Norman just laughed.

"We all know you're keeping something from us, but just can't think what, but we'll see you in the morning, bye."

Next morning after Jane had helped Betty bottle the milk, she went back home to get it in the fridge and then get ready for the seaside.

Jim had brought the 'Johnson Bus' to the village and parked next to the school, but realising everyone couldn't get in the living area, Ted had parked the minibus behind it. The villagers were amazed at what they had done and couldn't wait to see what the Johnsons had to say. They arrived about twenty minutes later and just stood there in amazement. "What do you think Norman?" asked Jim, "we just happened to find it one day."

"I can't believe you've done this just for us," replied Norman, "you are just wonderful people, thank you." Jack had decided to stay behind to keep an eye on the place and go another time, George had agreed to stay with him but the wives would go.

"Right, what are we waiting for, all aboard, Cleethorpes next stop," said Jim and off they went.

When they arrived at the seafront, they were surprised to see people already on the beach, it appeared to be two families, one with two children and one with three. They looked up in amazement as two buses pulled up and the two men started to approach them when Jim and Ted got out to meet them. "Good morning," said Ted, "you look surprised to see us, but why wouldn't you?"

"That could be an understatement," said the first man, "I'm Frank Darfield and this is Dave Ellis and we managed to survive in Grimsby."

"We have found some others out of town, but they don't get about much," said Dave, "but they supply us with meat and veg." One of the families had been farmers and had made use of a diesel generator much the same as Ted had done and got some batteries charged to get a car going, so they had transport.

The villagers started to get out, but Ted had to discuss mutants quickly so said, "Have you encountered any mutants since you emerged?"

"Yes, we have," said Frank, "but we have handled them with no problems."

"We also have," said Ted, "but they are good ones, and we've brought them with us, so don't be worried, they are excellent friends."

"OK Jan, you three can come out," said Jim and the 'cat folk' were introduced and greeted with caution, but hellos all round.

"Anyway, what's with the horse box?" said Frank, "don't tell me you've brought seaside donkeys."

"No," replied Ted, "but you've just met the felines, just take a deep breath and meet the equines."

"OK Jim, let them out," Jim lowered the tailgate and a family of four centaurs posed for reaction on their appearance. "Frank, Dave, I'd like you to meet Norman and Mary Johnson and their kids Tony and Beth, this is the most amazing family I have ever met." When the two had got their breath back it was handshakes all round with a couple of brief obvious questions, then down to the beach.

When the people on the beach saw them a couple of kids screamed but were soon assured by the villagers that they were friends. Soon there was a large group of people paddling and just enjoying the day with Norman and Tony giving the little one's rides and Mary gave a little girl a ride into the water and back.

Ted introduced Harry and it turned out he knew Frank's old bank manager as he used the same bank, but unfortunately had not survived. He went on to tell them about the village and Jack being more or less in charge and would hopefully come and see them sometime. Dave then said he had also been to the oil refinery and looked it over also noticing that someone had been.

He had been one of the production managers and realised that some tankers had gone but didn't want them anyway as they had no means of getting them going. Jim said they should keep in touch somehow and he could maybe help out sometime.

Well, the day continued with lots of discussion about the future and how to keep in touch, but at the moment it looked like being just by travel. Then Paul joined in and asked if they knew of anyone with a radio, but they hadn't at the moment, but Dave said he knew someone who did, but didn't know if he'd survived or not. So, Paul gave him his frequencies and hoped he had made it.

Frank said he had found a few more survivors in town but they had wanted to keep themselves to themselves for the time being, but he said now he can tell them about you and advise them to form a closer community as the villagers have done and hopefully keep in touch.

So goodbyes were said all round and everybody said it had been a great day, especially meeting other people, so it was time to load up and head back to the village.

When they got back home Jack was more than interested to know how it had gone. The men all got together and had good talk about everything they had learned and what they could do to improve communications with everyone they knew about.

So for the time being it looked like Paul was going to be busy on his radios, the more people they could contact the better. He had been in touch with the Sheffield contact again and discovered they had found more survivors and had started to form a close community to work together. They had thought about what Paul had told them about the village and decided to do the same. This was to be the same in Grimsby and Jack had said he would like to go over and meet them, but as they couldn't be contacted, they would just have to hope they were in when they went. Frank had given Ted his address, so they did know where to go.

Norman had thought about the cattle and realised they hadn't actually gone to the farm that had kept them as they had found them before they got there. So, he suggested to Jack that him and Ted should have a ride over to the farm and see what was happening if anything. As they hadn't much else to do they decided to go the next day and were more than pleased to find the farmers family there alive and well. As they didn't know each other they pleased to be met by other survivors. Jack explained about the cow, bull and calf Norman had found and wasn't surprised to hear, "That's where they went, I knew they had wandered off somewhere, but we have some more." Jack asked if they had goats which Norman had mentioned and was told they had and if they would like a pair that would be OK. "Tell you what," said Ted, "Norman has some pigs so we could swap you, two pigs for two goats." This was agreed, then it was time to tell them about the Johnsons. This was received with the usual caution but accepted and agreed to do the swap tomorrow. Jack was sure Norman would agree to the trade and he did. So next morning Ted met Norman at the farm and coupled up the 'taxi', then got the pigs in with plenty of room for Norman. On meeting the other farmer's family Norman was warmly greeted when he told them where he was from as the original Johnsons had known them.

So the swap was made and now the village could have goat's milk as well.

Meanwhile in Grimsby, Dave had been busy and found the chap with the radio had survived and encouraged him to get the thing working as the chap didn't realise there were others already on air. A few days later Paul's radio crackled into life. "Hello out there, can anyone hear me?" Paul picked up his 'mic' and replied. "Hi there, yes, this is Paul Saunders, where are you."

"Hi Paul," replied the voice, "this is Alec Foster in Grimsby, Dave Ellis gave me your frequency to get in touch, this is brilliant." So, contact with another group was established and they could now arrange meetings to discuss the future.

Jack was keen to go over there as he had missed out on the earlier trip, so him and Harry would arrange to go when Frank and Dave could get the others together. This was done and arrived at Frank's place mid-morning to be greeted by a small crowd. Harry introduced Jack who was received with a sign of respect from all. Now Frank had been doing a bit of research and not said anything to Harry when the meeting was arranged but had found another survivor as a surprise.

Frank stepped to the front and said, "Jack, we have only just met, but there is someone else I would like you to meet."

Then from the back of the crowd came a man who just walked up to Jack and said, "Hi pal, long time no see." Jack just stood a minute and said, "Good news just doesn't seem to stop for me, great to see you Nev." They just hugged each other for a while, Nev Greenwood was Jack's mate before being transferred over there a couple of years before the trouble. So that meeting went very well with lots of suggestions being made especially diesel as although there was enough for a few years, it wouldn't last for ever.

For power, they all had small generators, but Jack told them about what Paul and Ted had done with the large village generator and suggested they moved closer together and did something similar.

Then it was time to go home for Jack and Harry and there was lots to talk about on the way back to the village.

Norman had been spending a bit of time with Jan and family at the smallholding, he had given them advice on a couple of things they didn't know and brought them some more chickens. The old folk had also settle in with them and helped out on the land when they could.

Eric now had a better range of meats to deal with and Betty had fish when she could and asked George if he and one of the others would go fishing maybe once a week to keep a small stock. George readily agreed as milling was only required now and then.

Then one day Keith came to the village with another couple of survivors he had discovered, they both had families and were hoping to find somewhere in the village as Keith had suggested.

Norman was very pleased with the oats he had sown as the crop was growing well so as well as wheat, they would have a variety for breakfast.

So, it looked like things were eventually getting back to as near normal as was possible for now albeit in a bit of a primitive form. But it was something everyone had dreamed of when they took to the shelters, they had survived and thanked God they had. Over the radios they had discovered that there were more survivors in various places and were contacting each other regularly.

Well as we approach the end of our story we only come to the end of these written words.

All the survivors have said the same thing, they thought it was the end, but now it's a new beginning. Everyone said God had spared them for a reason and there would be no more violence, everyone would live in peace treat each other equally.